JAKE LOGAN

THE NECKTIE
PARTY

PLAYBOY
PAPERBACKS

Published simultaneously in the United States and Canada by Playboy Paperbacks, New York, New York. Printed in the United States of America. Library of Congress Catalog Card Number: 81-86259. First edition.

Books are available at quantity discounts for promotional and industrial use. For further information, write to Premium Sales, 1633 Broadway, New York, New York 10019.

ISBN: 0-867-21134-2

First printing August 1982.

1

Shotgun Slade was not exactly a good man, but he had a good wife, and in the eyes of some men she redeemed him. The number of saints in Virginia City in the years after the war was very small; it was a rough place in a rough time. Bill Fairweather was the first one to strike gold, although he lost four men to Indians when he brought the news of his strike back to the settlements. Bill's claim had been the first, but it wasn't the best, and pretty soon Bill was broke and happy again. The men who came after Bill were Cornish, Irish, and German miners, English remittance men, men with more than one name—men with more than ten names—men who'd kill you for your watch, who'd die rather than suffer an insult. They were mostly bachelors with an exaggerated respect for womankind and distant mothers. Maybe there weren't many saints in Virginia City, but each of the mothers of the men who toiled there was a saint, and one slurred them at the risk of gunplay.

The gold poured out of Virginia City, out of the prospect holes and the placer claims, out of the slurry boxes and pans. Gold dust was good as gold: $5 for a sack of spuds, $2 for a pick, $2 for a dozen eggs or a bottle of trade whiskey, $2 in the cribs behind the Bullwhacker saloon locked in the embrace of some

5

half-Indian whore—that's what gold bought in Virginia City.

One day, somebody would hit the mother lode. Maybe this summer. It could happen any time now. Prospecting was prime in the summer months, when there was plenty of water in the gulches, and this had been a wet spring. Men abandoned claims along Alder Gulch, abandoned proven producers to load up their pack mules. With a mysteriously stubborn expression on their faces, they set off to find the mother lode.

The gold in Alder Gulch was alluvial, which was what the mining men called bits of pure gold that had washed down from the mountains and lodged in the stream beds in gravel bars and banks. The biggest nuggets found in Virginia City were no bigger than a four-bit piece, but some of the best claims would keep a miner busy picking nuggets out of the black sand that remained when the sluice box was emptied. At $16 an ounce, men sometimes made $500 a day, which was close to a year's pay for a working man.

If they could keep it. If they could keep their claims. If they could keep their lives.

No doubt, some of the constant disputes about claim boundaries were genuine. Most were fairly outrageous. Most disputes were settled with guns or fists, and a big, fast man naturally had more luck as a miner than someone smaller and slower.

The claims weren't very large. The best, richest part of Alder Gulch wasn't half a mile long, and the small dugout tunnels and prospect holes didn't go farther up the bank than the creek's high-water mark. The claims were fifty by fifty or twenty by ten or ten by ten. Men dug bucketfuls of paydirt from their own claims and politely, carefully crossed two or three other men's claims on the way to the muddy creek where they owned part interest in a sluice box. They'd shovel their dirt into the screen and divert the water board, and the water would wash the lighter stuff away, leaving a great deal of black sand (magnetite), some flecks of pure yellow gold, and the odd sapphire or two. The sapphires weren't gem-quality, and men tossed them out with the other trash.

Work lasted from sunup to sundown. If you had a partner, he could sit up at night and make sure that nobody moved your claim markers or slipped a hand under your rough pillow for your poke as you slept. Of course, a partner might cheat you on the cut or cheat you on the work or outright kill you once your claim was played out. It had been known to happen.

Virginia City had started life as Varina City. It was named after the wife of Confederate president Jeff Davis. That was before a majority of Unionists arrived in town. They changed the name. A couple of men got shot for it.

They got shot for horses and women, too. They got shot because of promises broken and because of promises kept. They got shot for insults, delivered or offered. They died because of their politics and their daddies' politics. They died from penknife slashes and rat poison and old military bullets. They died from too close attention by Colonel Colt.

Most of them died for gold.

A couple years before, times were worse. The miners had a sheriff, one Henry Plummer by name. Plummer was always riding around the district, from Nevada City to Ophir, but he didn't seem to make a dent in the road agents, who were thick as fleas on a dog's back. He couldn't seem to find those boys, no matter how many posses he formed and sent out.

He had an office in the front of the territorial stable, a cubicle about horse-sized, with a rough window cut in the outside wall for air. Whenever he had prisoners too drunk to turn loose, he put them in the tack room and dropped the heavy steel bar down across the door, and they were snug there.

The town wriggled along Alder Gulch, giving the creek plenty of space. Nobody wanted to build buildings on paydirt, and so most of them were situated on old, worked-out claims. The Virginia City Opera House was set on a claim that had yielded $30,000, and the Fairweather Inn was set on the site of Bill Fairweather's exhausted claim.

Virginia City had a handful of two-story structures, fifty one-story buildings, and several hundred shacks, soddies, and holes in the ground with canvas for a roof and a stovepipe sticking through the mud bank at the rear.

While Sheriff Plummer rode around with his pals, looking for outlaws, it got dangerous on all the trails around Virginia City. The road agents would kill a man for his horse, and if he had any dust at all, he wouldn't live past his first campsite. Some men hired other men to accompany them, figuring that two or three guns were better than one. Plummer's deputies were usually called upon as bodyguards. Nobody saw these men again. The deputies said, "Sure, sure. We left old Gus at the fork of Bozeman Trail, and he was healthy as could be." But how come old Gus never wrote back from St. Louis like he'd promised so faithfully he was going to do, and how come Gus's family fired off letters by the newly established Pony Express to the gold camps, asking whether anyone had any knowledge of the whereabouts of their husband, son, or father?

The deputies would say, "That Bozeman Trail is awful rough. Many a good man has fallen on the Bozeman Trail."

This went on until some of the local citizens were asked to swallow a bit too much. Citizens had insisted that Plummer hire a new deputy, an honest young man named Christopher Dobbs. A week after he'd been sworn in, two of the older deputies took him outside from MacArdle's saloon, one on each arm. Once outside, the guns talked.

"It was an accident," one deputy said.

"He drew first," another said.

Henry Plummer was out of town.

The good citizens met that night, about fifty of them, and said that the only way they were going to have any safety in Virginia City—no, by God, in the entire territory—would be if honest men banded together and took matters into their own hands. They all shook hands. They agreed to send warnings to the bad hats and scoundrels, one warning per bad hat.

NOTICE

The honest man has nothing to fear from justice. All others saddle up.

Signed,
The Committee of Vigilance

3-7-77

Naming themselves the Committee of Vigilance was the idea of some men who'd been in San Francisco in '49, when similar committees had been a scourge to the ungodly and slow to escape.

As soon as they started holding necktie parties, these men got to be famous simply as the vigilantes, and the "3-7-77" got known all through the territory as their signature.

They put the two deputies up on a platform and threw the noose over the running beam outside the territorial stable where Plummer had his office. They asked whether the deputies had anything to say. It turned out that they did. With the nooses brushing their faces, the deputies mentioned their mothers. One said, "Oh, give me a week just so I can get my last message to my sainted mother."

This appeal was more effective than one might think. Most of the miners were more interested in gold-digging than hanging men, and a mother was a good excuse to forget the whole thing.

A little guy sat on the fence, watching the whole affair, a quiet fellow who carried a shotgun somewhat taller than himself. This shotgun had its butt on the ground and leaned against his shoulder, even though he was perched a couple of feet in the air. He was picking at his fingernails.

"Ask them how much time they gave Chris Dobbs," he said.

With that sort of reasoning, the miners made a quick job of it.

The next deputy decided to clear his conscience before God. He named all the other road agents he could think of and a few men he thought were just plain evildoers. With his partner's legs jerking beside him, he said, "Stop your kickin', pal. I'll be in hell as soon as you will."

They strung him up, too, and others. The little man, X. Beidler, became the vigilantes' advance man. Beidler would come into a camp and sniff around for a month or so, and then suddenly a spate of crudely printed warnings would appear, and the bad hats would either run for their lives or dance with the rope of thirteen knots.

It got so that when X. Beidler and Beamis, his assistant, rode into town, the local ruffians selected themselves out and rode away. It saved trouble that way. When Beidler didn't have members of the original Vigilance Committee to help him, he created a new branch office. Since all the camps were just as tough as

Virginia City and there were lawbreakers to go around for everybody, Beidler had no particular difficulty forming new branches of the vigilantes. Sometimes Beidler and Beamis just did the job themselves.

Beidler said that he had decided to quit hunting gold and start hunting sons of bitches. That was the only explanation he ever gave for becoming the vigilantes' advance man. Prominent judges and attorneys formed the vigilantes' backbone. Beidler was their dog.

In those days, it was quite the thing to be a member of the Committee of Vigilance and perhaps one of the better ways to avoid getting hanged by mistake. You'd ride out by night or by day, and since the road agents were an unimaginative lot and fairly unskilled, they weren't hard to catch. Generally, hoping to save their souls from hell, they confessed to many crimes before they swung. Sometimes the vigilantes let them take time for a brief letter to their sainted mothers. They always gave them time for a short prayer.

Both the vigilantes and the road agents were young. It was no country for old men.

Plummer was just thirty when they hanged him, and the men who rode under him were in their early twenties. Most of them were garden-variety ruffians: foulmouthed, foul-tempered, mostly drunk, mostly unwashed, mostly lazy, and not very bright. On occasion, the vigilantes hanged a man who was a cut above the others. They caught young Dave Gallagher hiding out in a barn with another man, one Burkhardt, whom they were looking for. There were twenty vigilantes and two road agents, and it was getting dark. The vigilantes wanted to get it over with quickly. They talked it over among themselves. Gallagher was known as a promising young man, recently from the East. It was known that he was literate and sometimes composed miners' letters home for them. He was thought to have come from

Illinois or Indiana and was too young to have fought in the war. He was just sowing his wild oats: robbing men and stealing their horses.

The vigilantes couldn't help that. They decided to hang both men on the spot rather than escort them all the way back to Virginia City for a miners' court.

It was easier said than done. Satisfactory ways of hanging men aren't always available, and the inside of the barn had no accessible beams to drape a rope around. A couple of men tied Burkhardt's hands, and one vigilante scrambled up the wall and passed the rope through an angle brace. Then all three men got on the end of the rope and dragged on it. They got their victim's feet off the ground. He kicked for quite a while—twenty minutes or so—and made awful noises and voided himself. The vigilantes agreed that they'd made a botch of it. Throughout, Gallagher waited his turn. He was very still, and his face was the color of spilled milk.

It was already dark. The vigilantes weren't in so much of a hurry, and they hoped to do a better job by the boy.

The barn was used to feed cattle during the winter months. Although it was springtime and the fragrant mounds of hay were gone, haymaking equipment was everywhere. Pitchforks, a horse-drawn rake, and a hay-wagon were parked in one empty bay. Far above the floor was a small platform, no more than fifteen feet across, with a great hole in the center where they unloaded the wagons.

They pushed the boy up the high ladder ahead of them. They fastened one end of the rope to the top rung of the ladder and had the boy sit down on the platform. Up there the stink from the man they'd killed was pretty bad. They climbed down the ladder and looked up to where Gallagher sat on a mound of loose hay. They looked at him; he looked at them.

Gallagher said, "Since I have not had the honor of

being hanged before, I don't know how to go about it. Do I jump or slide?"

"Jump," they yelled, and he did.

Afterward it became a joke among the vigilantes; a joke nobody shared who hadn't ridden out on a necktie party. Vigilantes would gather in the saloons and have a drink and make a mock toast and say, "Jump or slide?" Somebody would respond, properly, "Jump." There was laughter on all sides, drinks for the house.

That was a couple of years ago. These days Virginia City considered itself fairly well behaved, and the vigilantes, if they were busy, were busy in some of the newer camps, where the miners were not much better than animals. Virginia City was prospering. Most of the functioning prospect holes even had their own johnny houses, which was a definite sign of progress, particularly on unlit pathways at night. X. Beidler was back in town, having returned from one of his tours, but he was no more talkative than he had been and didn't seem to be organizing any necktie parties. In Virginia City toward the end of July, the main work was mining, and the main hope was still the mother lode.

John Slocum hung out with Shotgun Slade most of the morning, until Slade got so drunk that Slocum got bored. He left Slade drinking in MacArdle's and went over to the Bullwhacker, looking for a friendly game. He found more than he'd anticipated.

In those days John Slocum was tough and tan, and the muscles of his shoulders were hard as bone. He'd worked out one claim and sunk most of what he'd made into a new, supposedly richer claim at the head of the gulch. Before he bought the hundred by fifty foot claim, he'd dug a couple buckets of gravel and washed it with his own pan and found color: grains of gold, about the size of coarse salt, and one nugget the size of a kernel of white corn. John Slocum owned $800, gold weighed and assayed as a service by the Yellow Kid, who worked the bar at the Bullwhacker. Slocum had dug the gold from his piece of sandbar, a shovelful at a time, and panned it out by hand, swirling every ounce of it because he hadn't trusted anyone enough to go in on a sluice box with him. His old claim had been very narrow and very shallow. When he got through the sandbar, there was no gold in the gravel substratum, and he sold the claim to a Chinese man for $50. If Slocum knew the Chinese, he'd be scrupulously honest and work his fingers raw on a claim every inch of which had been dug and sifted by the other man. And the Chinese man would make money, too.

Slocum paid $800 for the new claim and kept the $50 for luck. The first day he made $30, the second day $10. The third day he found plenty of magnetite but no gold. The man who'd sold him the claim had taken his money and traveled on. Some said that he was going out to Seattle; others said St. Joe. Slocum wanted to talk to him. Slocum was particularly interested in the night before he sampled the claim, when the man had been seen loading an old smooth-bore shotgun with bits of gold and quartz instead of shot. He'd been seen firing that shotgun into the reef that he and Slocum panned the next day. Slocum was pretty calm about the whole thing, just mad enough to kill. He just walked off the claim. Not even the Chinese man wanted it. "Claim is salted, mister," he said.

Slocum washed up in the muddy water of the creek and went into MacArdle's, where he and Shotgun Slade had a few drinks—Slade more than a few. Slocum liked Jack Slade when he was sober or half drunk, because he was funny and didn't give a damn for anything under God's heaven. Except his wife, Bonnie. Bonnie he loved dearly, and when he was drunk and most foul, he never mentioned her or cast a slur or insulted her or said anything to indicate that he wasn't the luckiest man on earth to have captured such a bride.

Jack was okay for a sidekick on the trail, or you might want to hire him for a backup gun or to guard a bullion shipment, but you didn't want to drink with him once he got past that certain point. If you were a Reb, he'd talk about traitors and rebels and turncoats and that scum Robert E. Lee. If you were a Unionist, he'd say that Abe Lincoln got just what was coming to him from John Booth, and wasn't it a shame the killers missed the Secretary of State? He had a way about him, Jack did.

When he started looking surly, John Slocum left him, went down the street, and run into his first piece of good luck in weeks. He'd no more than sat down at the table in the Bullwhacker, where two other men were playing nickel-dime blackjack, when a burly miner pulled out a chair, clapped his hands together, and said, "Boys, my name is Murphy. I'm a miner by trade and a gambler by inclination, and I'm too rich right now to do any mining, though I aim to get out and find the mother lode. I got my jack donkey out front with a full grubstake and every provision under the sun. I had me three of the ladies at Mother Sue's house of soiled doves, and they was more soiled after than before I came to them. I been drunk for a week in a row now, and I got to tell you, the only thing that prevents me from goin' out and finding that mother lode is this poke of gold." He tossed a heavy sack on the table. "Because every time I look at this gold, I say to myself that any man would be a fool to go mining when he has plenty of this stuff to keep him right here." He winked. His big eyelid sliding over his eyeball invited complicity. "So I aim to walk out of here a gambler, with every cent you boys have, or a miner, happy and dead broke. What'll it be?"

Slocum said, "Yellow Kid? Bring a bottle over here. Bring the scales."

The Yellow Kid had brilliantined hair, thick and glossy as melted lard. His hair started out the morning black, but by nightfall it was faintly brown, almost blond.

There wasn't so much cash money out here, and nobody cared for scrip. Men trusted gold more than the government's promises to pay, and the state and national banks were even riskier, although a few of the notes —notably the beehive notes of the National Bank of Salt Lake City—were thought to be as good as metal.

Every saloon, every mercantile, even the opera house, owned a set of scales. One drink was a pinch of dust. A bottle was three pinches. Anything more was weighed.

The Yellow Kid was named for his habit of running his hands through his thick greasy hair whenever he weighed gold.

"Bring a deck of cards," Slocum urged him. "Fresh faces, fresh deck."

The Yellow Kid performed that service, too, laying the unopened deck at the miner's elbow. Murphy was a ruddy, cheerful man in his late twenties. His eyes sparkled. "Here's to you," he said to the other players. "Since we won't like each other once I have your money or you have mine, I'll take this chance to drink your health."

Slocum grinned. He could take a liking to a man like this. John Slocum was a few years younger than the big Irish miner and taller, too, topping Murphy's five foot six by a good six inches. The casual observer would have guessed that the miner outweighed Slocum by fifty pounds, but he would have been wrong. Without his boots, John Slocum weighed in at two hundred pounds. Muscle is heavier than fat. Slocum's eyes were green. Right now they were the green of mischief, but they could get cold and even heartless, and then they flared deep. A man was wise at those times to talk softly and walk wide around him.

Slocum's hands were too rough for the iron he carried. He wore one Colt Navy on his left hip, ready for a cross draw, and had another stuck in his belt. His guns were well cared-for. The ebony butts shone from light oil, and the hammers of the pistols were held by a thong. Most miners carried pistols on the right hip, and most favored the Army's covered holster, because you might want to wear your pistol day in and day out for a year before you had to use it, and so you protected it from the weather. Slocum's rig was a gunfighter's rig. His weapons had to be checked and the charges drawn every time it rained or snowed. His weapons had to be cared for very tenderly and very often. For all this care he gained one advantage: speed. His pistols were so fast that they looked fast. They looked like another presence in his belt, an invitation to try your luck, and a threat. In Virginia City, only Shotgun Slade wore his pistols like Slocum. A couple of years ago there'd been quite a few men in town with gunfighter's rigs, but most of them had been hanged.

A pistol shot. Another one. The Yellow Kid went to the door.

"It's that damn Slade. He's shooting up MacArdle's place. He's standing outside and shooting MacArdle's glass." The Kid laughed. "Oh, that'll make him burn. Second time this month he's had to put boards across his window while he freighted in new glass."

From some obscure loyalty, Slocum said, "Slade always pays up."

The Yellow Kid answered sourly. "Sure he does. But while you wait for his dust, you got to board up your windows, and you lose a little trade then, I'll tell you, because nobody likes to sit in a saloon where he can't take a look-see outside and keep an eye on his horse. And then you got to find Slade, and I'll tell you, some brave men have flinched then." He poured himself a short drink of whiskey. The Yellow Kid was remembering. "And then you got to catch Jack when he's sober, which ain't so damn awful easy as it might sound. You got to catch him before noon, because he passes out about 3 P.M. and starts again when he wakes up, because he's got such a hangover. You go up to him in the morning and say, 'Jack, how about that window?' and he doesn't remember. He doesn't remember a damn thing. He gives you a look like you're trying to rob him, and he drawls, 'Let's just sit down, partner, and have a friendly drink and talk about it.' Well, what are you going to do? Of course, you sit down and take a drink of whiskey, and you take a big drink, because if you take a small one he'd be offended, and by God, you don't want to have him mad at you. No, sir."

The Yellow Kid rinsed his glass and put it behind the bar. Two more shots sounded down the street, but he didn't go to the door to check this time. "So you sit there and drink your drink, and he's puttin' away two to your one. Well, first off, you got to be sociable, which means listening to him tell stories about the goddamn Overland stage company where he used to manage the 'by-God toughest station on the godforsaken route,' though you might have heard this tale a time or two. If you're real lucky, he'll tell you about Little Jimmy Eads. That's a nice thing to hear about in the morning. Then, sometime after you've drunk your second glass of whiskey, he'll ask you about the damage he's done. That whiskey! God damn, no wonder he likes to hooraw the town. He drinks nothin' but trade whiskey, and it's raw stock. I know. I make it. I sell it, but I don't know many men not down on their luck who'll drink it. Gunpowder, tobacco plugs, some iron nails in the barrel for body, and there, gentlemen, after you add your pure raw rotgut whiskey, you have the delicate flavor of trade whiskey."

"Kid, I didn't know you were a poet," Slocum said.

"If he hasn't yet started to get mean, you get to tell

Slade how much he owes you. You know how he is. You never know what the hell he's going to do, because he's no more predictable than a damn she-grizzly. He's liable to go any which way. You find yourself sayin', 'Well, Jack. It wasn't so bad. You shot up my back mirror and a dozen bottles on the back bar. Oh, let's see. It comes to, let's see now. . . . Will $10 be too much?' "

"You bein' scared doesn't have anything to do with it," Slocum said. "So long as he pays off."

"Oh, he pays off, all right. Got to give him that, but I won't give him one more damn inch. After a morning wasted, he'll pay off the damage you undercharged him for because you were afraid he'd do you like he did Little Jimmy Eads. Hell, that damn mirror alone was worth $50. Sure, he pays up."

Murphy said, "I come by here to play poker."

Slocum said that Murphy was a man after his own heart, and they would play stud or draw, table stakes, no check and raise. That suited everybody. It was the standard rules.

Slocum asked the Yellow Kid to bring him a beer. The beer was Centennial beer from Last Chance Gulch, and it was pretty good and cold so long as they kept the sawdust moist. Centennial beer was two pinches the bottle, twice what whiskey cost. The beer had to be freighted a hundred miles down the Madison Valley, and any damn fool could make whiskey.

Slocum put every cent he owned on the table, which was how he liked to play. Play full, don't hold back, and make no provision for failure. Take your beatings when you're beat. In his young life he'd learned that much.

He'd fought on the wrong side in the war, fought under slick old Joe Johnson in the mountains near his home in Georgia. He'd fought with General Jo Shelby's irregulars, who were only a half step better than the murderous guerrillas Quantrill led. He'd fought for

Quantrill, too, although he never spoke about that time, not even to men he trusted.

He had lost it all in the war. His father and mother died while he was away; his brother died at Pickett's impossibly brave charge at Cemetery Ridge. Still, a man had to have something, some hope. That's what he thought when he came home to the overgrown acres generations of Slocums had farmed—Slocum's Stand.

There wasn't much left when John Slocum returned from the war, but the hope of seeing it again had sustained him through many a long night and strengthened him to go into battle again and again. He didn't suppose too many men lived through the war who'd seen the action he had, but that was the kind of thinking a smart man avoids, because you naturally start figuring that your luck must be stretched too thin by now or that you are running out your string, and then you start to shade the odds, you start to weasel, you lose your fine edge—and your life.

Slocum's Stand was abandoned because he'd fled from Georgia after a battle he'd fought to hold it. He fought the battle and lost the war, fought two men and killed them both. One was a federal judge.

Maybe he was better off without anything to be tied to. Maybe he was better off alone. At least he didn't have so much to worry him. It didn't make too much difference what he did from day to day, and if he took a mind to, he could ride right out of Virginia City tonight, just like he'd ridden out of a hundred similar towns since the war.

"I said $5. Kings say $5." Murphy was impatiently pinching dust into the pan of the scale.

"And five." Slocum had a six in the hole to go with the pair he had showing. It wasn't the sort of hand a man with a pair of kings should bet into, and Slocum nearly folded when Murphy raised him right back. But some instinct warned him to stay. "Call."

The two kings were all Murphy had, and he shrugged and smiled a big smile. One of the other players, a tinhorn from the cut of him, coughed, took a drink of whiskey, and leaned forward like a vulture on a branch.

Slocum loosened his belt and called for another beer. It looked to be a long afternoon. Already the backs of his hands were tingling. Murphy was going to throw his money away with both hands until it was all gone. He'd interrupt this process with good play when he changed his mind, but he'd go right back into the slide before his smart play took hold. He'd win only to prove to himself that he could win if he wanted to, which of course he didn't, because he had larger matters on his mind: mining matters, traveling matters, the mother lode. Murphy was offering a sacrifice here. Without the best grace in the world, he would throw all his good money after bad until he was shorn, humbled, and clean again. John Slocum had seen it before more than once. The lamb had come to the slaughter.

It was hard to think of this big, tough Irish miner as a lamb to the slaughter, but even the tinhorn had picked it up. Murphy wasn't betting nickels now; he was betting from his poke.

They set the gold tray between them while they bet. The winner took the tray and dribbled it into his poke. If anyone doubted the value of a pinch—too thinly held in too-slender fingers—then they used the scale, but its presence was a fair guarantee that nobody would pull anything too raw.

"Twenty-five dollars," the miner said. He sat hunched, glaring at his cards like they were an enemy's face.

Down the street Slade let loose another string of shots, five this time.

"Call." Slocum thought that his ace high was as good as anything on the table, and he was right. Soon he'd try

some outrageous bluff and submit to being called. He'd
throw his cards down in disgust, and the others would
see his poor cards and think him a fool. In some later
hand, they'd remember that to their disadvantage, but for
now he just wanted to build up his stake because a man
with $50—no, $120 now—couldn't hope to challenge a
man with a poke that must have weighed five pounds.

Gold pokes were made from the finest deerskin. The
inner pouch was belly skin from a fawn, and the outer
pouch was a doeskin because it was a little softer and
smoother than buckskin. The pokes sat before their
owners, complaisant as idols. The Irish miner called for
another bottle of whiskey. Slocum whistled soundlessly.
Murphy meant to get drunk, too, so that he'd have
another reason for throwing it away.

The Yellow Kid brought the bottle. There were no
other customers in the bar. "Mind if I sit in?"

"Yes," the tinhorn said. "I hate a five-man poker
game," meaning that he didn't want to share the pick-
ings.

Slocum was a little disgusted by all of this. He thought
he'd give the Irishman a chance. It wouldn't do a bit of
good, but he'd feel better for it. It was his deal, and he
laid his hands on the cards. "Slade again?" he asked.

"Yep. He'll have his horse in the barroom before dark,
I'll wager." The Yellow Kid wasn't offended by the
tinhorn's refusal. He'd wait for his chance. The Kid had
plenty of patience and plenty of dust, too. He was
pleased to make himself agreeable. "You ever meet that
wife of his, Bonnie?"

Slocum nodded. He kept one hand on the cards and
sipped his tepid beer.

"I can't see what a beautiful woman like her sees in a
man like him."

Slocum drawled, "Women's love's the most democratic thing there is. Likely Judas had a girl that loved him."

"Cut the palaver," the miner said. "Those cards are hot."

The tinhorn looked satisfied because he'd been meaning to say the same thing but couldn't think of a way to do it.

Slocum looked surprised. "They ain't hot for you," he remarked mildly. "She's been with him since he had that stage station for the Overland. Met in Utah, she said once."

"She's been comin' into town regular. Learning her letters."

Slocum shrugged. "She's got a talent to improve herself."

"Reminds me of young Dave Gallagher," the Yellow Kid said. "Jump or slide? Hah."

The Yellow Kid hadn't been with the vigilantes when they hanged Plummer. He'd missed all the hangings in Last Chance Gulch and Nevada City. The Yellow Kid liked to ally himself with the successful. He had an eye to the future, when membership in the Committee of Vigilance might really mean something in the territory. The Yellow Kid had been so successful with his one invention, his golden hair, that he forgot that he was a seedy and rather unsuccessful saloonkeeper. The Yellow Kid was the kind of man others tell one story about. He wasn't worth two.

He had as much chance of getting into the Committee of Vigilance as John Slocum did, which was none.

The miner knew the joke and didn't think that it was funny, and he said so. If he hadn't been ready to lose every dime he'd grubbed out of the hills with pick and shovel and his bare hands, he'd have kept his opinions to himself, but a man can say anything if he's willing to lose everything. "I mean, what's so damn funny about a kid dancin' on the end of a rope?"

"Can't say I find it too hilarious," Slocum noted. Maybe he could give this man a chance. Slocum liked to play poker and never would turn down a foolish bet. It was a point of pride. But he didn't have to like the foolish bets. "Can't say I think a lot about this 3-7-77 business."

The Yellow Kid got stuffy. Those who try hardest for what they can't attain are often stuffy about it. "Mr. Beidler is a credit to any community," he said.

"If the town's got a hemp factory in it."

The Yellow Kid climbed off his high horse. The lower the man, the higher the horse. "It probably ain't wise to go off talkin' that way," he said.

"Hell, ain't nobody going to make me the guest of honor at a necktie party," Slocum said. "I had a run-in with X. Beidler once, in a town called Blue Rock in the Crazy Mountains. Oh, we scratched at each other like cats in a box. I didn't shoot him. He didn't string me up. That's how it is. I'm no road agent and never was and got nothing to fear so long as I ain't. Isn't that about right?"

"That's right. Mr. Beidler is an honest man. He wouldn't string a man up for nothing."

"Good. Now, I'm sure my friend here wants to play again, but I mean to tell you all about Little Jimmy Eads. Jimmy was hot-tempered and quick with his hands and had a taste for the fast life. The Overland put Jack Slade in the stage station because stock was getting rustled off. Every time they brought in a new bunch of stage remounts, they'd be gone within a month. The station was midway between Thermopolis and the start of the Bozeman Trail, and a man and his horse could vanish in that country like the earth swallowed them up. Jack Slade went after the rustlers just like he'd been hired to do, and he performed some crude operations on those he caught. Well, most rustlers went after easier prey and hitting the immigrant trains on the Bozeman. Little Jimmy Eads watched the horses at the stage station get fat and fatter, and Jimmy's pals would tell him how well old Jack had been doing with that stage station, and wasn't it a shame how them that had, got; and them that didn't, didn't get any. Little Jimmy started taking those horses himself. He'd slip into the station in the wee hours and the dark of the moon and just kind of ease himself up on some horse's back and give her a kick, and she's jump right out of that corral, which was just a four-foot corral, just a little thing. Now, Little Jimmy wasn't known for his brains. He had figured out that Jack Slade wouldn't be able to sit up all night watching his horses and do a day's work the next day. Not for too long, anyway. And Jimmy was a fine rider and a lightweight rider, and he didn't fear bein' rode down by Jack Slade, who is a heavier man." Another rattle of gunfire down the street; more breaking glass. "Jimmy figured he'd just come around and slip into that corral whenever he felt like it and take one of those fat fine horses and sell it in Thermopolis for eating money. He got away with four of them."

The Yellow Kid poured Slocum a drink, because he was still hoping to sit in when the game resumed.

"The very next time Little Jimmy jumped a fine, fat horse out of the corral, he hit the top rail, because Slade had raised that corral three feet so that Jimmy couldn't jump it anymore."

Slocum drank the drink.

"What happened?" the miner asked in spite of himself.

"Slade tied Little Jimmy to a corral post and took the day off. He started drinking, and as he started drinking, he started to get a little mean, so he'd go out and shoot a piece off Little Jimmy. There were a fair number of pieces of Little Jimmy, more than you might expect in such a small man, and he lasted until sunset. Slade says he never got so drunk in his life, but he never missed what he was aiming at. Now, partner"—Slocum directed his gaze toward the Irish miner—"if you want to lose all your money before you go looking for that mother lode, I'm right here to accommodate you."

The miner gaped. He firmed up, and some color flared in his cheeks. "Play cards," he said.

2

"You can tell a man by how much he can hold and still hit his mark," Jack Slade said. His Remington cracked and put a neat hole between Lillie Langtry's left eye and her right. The left eye was more blue than the right because the painting had been done by an itinerant Italian sign painter with a thirst bigger than his talent. Lillie also had a faint but noticeable leer on her thickly painted lips; and although it may have been a trick of the light, her eyes were very slightly crossed. On her face and her yellow gown, patches of tape were glued over the bullet holes other drunks had made in Lillie. Lillie was only one of Jacob MacArdle's pretentions. As in the other saloons in Virginia City, the ceiling of MacArdle's place was stamped tin, painted white, but MacArdle, with a ladder and one helper, had laboriously outlined each of the tiny tin squares in black. The effect was like a honeycomb and made some men nervous, because in a poor light those squares could look very much like holes, and who knows what can crawl out of holes when the DTs are upon you?

MacArdle's carefully painted squares kept most of the worst drunks out of the joint, which MacArdle didn't object to, since he was after the quality trade. Virginia City's lawyers, doctors, the wheelwright, two judges, the surveyor Breckinridge, and the German assayer—all did their drinking and socializing in the place, and MacArdle greeted them all by name. If not social equals, they were equals in the all-male society of the saloon.

MacArdle didn't allow any of the soiled doves into his place and no damn pistoleros, either. He blocked the door to uninformed newcomers in their feathers and finery, barring their paths with an imperious arm and hard words. If he'd tried that trick when Jack Slade wanted a drink, probably he'd have been ridden down. Very often Slade got up on his horse and wouldn't dismount to do his drinking.

His pistol roared again, and another hole appeared in Miss Langtry, just where her breast bulged under her extremely decorous gown. Jack Slade could hit what he aimed at, no doubt about it. He'd skipped the war and regretted little of it: the orders, the marching, the grub, the "yes, sir" and the "no, sir." It was not for Mrs. Slade's favorite boy, Jackie. But he had missed the opportunity to shoot as many men as he wanted to, an opportunity the war had offered many other gunmen. But Jack was only twenty-five and had plenty of time left to get into a war if he wanted to. Surely there'd be a good fuss with the Spanish someday, or the Mexicans. No good American had ever forgotten what the Mexicans did at the Alamo, if it served them not to forget, and it had served Jack Slade a time or two.

Slade was an average good-looking kind of gent: dark brown hair that he combed over to one side like a wave breaking and gray eyes that laughed or snarled and seemed to have no other expressions. His eyes were smallish and set deep in his skull. His heavy slab-sided cheeks had confused many men, who had judged him as fleshy and slow, which was the sort of mistake Jack let you make only once. His arms were heavy and shorter than average, but plenty long enough to reach the

Remington Double Action pistols he preferred. He wore his pistols on top of his gray-fawn vest in a cross-draw rig that John Wesley Hardin was said to have favored.

Slade never knew Hardin. Slade had been born in St. Louis and had gone west as soon as he was old enough to escape the orphanage. He'd never been to Texas, and Hardin was in jail, anyway. Still, he'd have liked to meet Hardin. Bet he could have killed him. Most of the thirty men Hardin had killed were niggers and spics, and they didn't really count. Only white men counted. Not Indians, either. Slade stared into his drink. He'd asked for and gotten his usual heavy water tumbler with four ounces of MacArdle's trade whiskey. Although it was the custom to keep your poke or cash on the bar as a sign of good faith, there was no poke before Jack Slade. He never paid when he was drinking. He paid on the delayed-payment plan.

Slade had chased all the other customers out of MacArdle's saloon. Nobody likes to drink or converse when the man sitting down at the bar might decide to blow up your drink glass at any moment or cut the end off your cigar. Jack Slade never hit anybody by accident. That was a boast he made frequently. So far as anybody knew, Jack was as good as his word, but still. . . .

"Why don't you do your drinking somewhere else?" MacArdle asked. MacArdle had both hands clasped behind his back. He was bouncing on the soles of his feet, and his neck was outthrust like the neck of a galloping chicken. He was behind the bar of a saloon he privately called "my pride and joy." His feet were bouncing on the broken glass of the whiskey bottles Slade had blown up, one bottle at a time.

"Hah. I got you to talk this time. I win. You-all bring me more whiskey and a beer chaser this time. Okay, partner?"

One day MacArdle would meet Jack at the front door

of his saloon with a ten-gauge in his arms and a look of pure pleasure on his pinched features. Jack Slade knew that.

On that day Slade would kill him because MacArdle didn't know when to pose. Jack Slade understood posing. You posed when you were drunk and up in the saddle or bellied up to the bar and didn't give a damn about anything and couldn't remember anything except how you'd always been kind to your family and friends and the women you loved. Where was Bonnie? Slade looked around for her.

"Why don't you drink somewhere else?" MacArdle hissed the word "else." His teeth were clenched so tight that his jaw hurt.

"Oh, hell. You'd miss me, Mac. Wouldn't know what to do with all that ugliness in you if you didn't have me to pin it on."

He quaffed the drink straight, and it made him cough. "Damn. You serve fine hooch," he said, admiring his empty glass. MacArdle refilled it with ill grace. "Yep, I figure I'm doing you a big favor. If you was a married man, your wife, she'd thank me, too. I come in here every month or so. I don't come in more than that, mind you. I start out drinking somewhere else, and I don't come in here before I'm about half lit and all broke." He dipped a fat red tongue in the glass and wiggled it. He sucked his tongue. "You serve fine whiskey. My absence gives you a chance to get the place fixed up nice, patch poor ol' Lil there." He gestured at the portrait of Miss Langtry.

Despite MacArdle's attempts with the patches, he wasn't the artist the Italian had been. The paints, which had been in an unheated shed behind the saloon through the winter, had gone all grainy, and so each patch was almost like a blemish, much rougher than the original.

"You get Lil fixed up and your usual bunch of

high-falutin' tenderfeet in here talkin' the way they do, so solemn and all."

MacArdle was furious, and he was fascinated, too, as always, but he was readier to listen than he had been before, because he had set the wheels in motion. Those were the very words he used to describe what he'd done. He'd set the wheels in motion.

"So you get thirty days of makin' money and fixin' up the damage, and as the end of that month comes close, you're countin' the days, because, Jesus, MacArdle, I'm punctual. Ain't I punctual?"

"Oh, you have a fine sense of timing, indeed."

"So that's what you got to be grateful for, MacArdle. Hell. Without me, you'd have nothin' to worry about. Now, I know men like you, so mean and pinched you'd do for the belt buckle on a snake. You sit amongst your pals like a man with the consumption. They pay attention to you because you're so damn sick. Well, I'm why you're sick, MacArdle, and I'm the only reason anybody in this plaguey town will pay attention to you."

"Oh, thank you, Mr. Slade."

"Don't mention it. Don't mention it, my boy. How long I been coming in here?"

Wordlessly MacArdle went into his cash drawer. He extracted a sheaf of bills and examined a long one carefully. "I first replaced the back bar mirror in October of last year. You'd been in here once or twice before."

"I told you I was sorry about that mirror. I paid for it, didn't I?"

"You did. It took until the passes were open in May for a replacement to be shipped."

"Well, I ain't shot it out, have I?" he asked petulantly.

The little bar owner looked around his empty establishment and sighed. "You've occupied your attention with other favorite objects," he said.

"Well, I ain't brought my horse in since, have I?"

"Not in some little while." A look of mild surprise appeared on the owner's saturnine face.

"Not since there was snow on the ground," Slade explained cheerfully. "I remember because his shoes was all slippery, and I was half afraid that horse'd go down and cut himself on the glasses I'd shot up."

"How exactly do you make your money, Mr. Slade?"

"I'm a man of what you might call independent means."

There'd been talk about Jack Slade that some of the richer small immigrant wagons were robbed and looted by a white man who left Indian sign. That was the talk around the territory, but it wasn't loud, and most men of good sense thought that it was a possibility but not a probability.

MacArdle leaned over his wide walnut bar and poured Jack another drink. "Don't suppose you'd like to come work for me?" he asked in an insinuating tone. "You could sit on that stool beside the door on a Saturday night with your shotgun, and if any of the boys should get real rough, you'd just put them out."

"That's white of you," Slade said. He drank the drink and held out his glass. "Yep. I'm right glad to see you hold me no hard feelings. It's all in fun. Like I said, it's all in fun." He stared into his glass and didn't see the smile flicker across MacArdle's face. Wheels in motion.

"Did I ever tell you how I did for Little Jimmy Eads?"

"Oh, yes. You certainly did. On several occasions you've regaled me with that particular story."

"Regaled? Regaled? Now, that's what I like about you, MacArdle. You're such a swell. Now, without my turning around, I want you to tell me something."

"Yes?"

"That Centennial‐ beer poster on your back wall. . . ."

"Yes?"

"I don't remember. Is it all capital letters?"

"No."

"Then somebody should dot the 'i.' "

Both Slade's elbows were on the bar as he spoke, and his little gray eyes were locked on MacArdle's softer ones. When MacArdle's brain registered, then and only then did Slade act. He came off the bar, flipping to the side. His double-action Remington spat once, and the Centennial beer poster was marked.

MacArdle didn't care. He'd had to plead with the brewery salesman for this long, heavy tin sign because wagon space was too precious to waste carrying advertising materials when the wagons could carry more profitable items. No other saloon in Virginia City had a poster on its back wall, but MacArdle just smiled. "Nice shooting," he said.

"I'm a better man drunk on my feet than many men cold sober," Slade said.

He laid his Remington on the bar, punched the empty out through the loading gate, and inserted a new wax-tipped bullet after holding it up to the light, looking for imperfections that could make it fly less than true. Slade had owned the Remingtons for a couple of years and was used to them. Like most real gunmen, he was quite indifferent to the guns he used, so long as they worked. They had no more romance to him than a shaving mug or stirrups. The bright fancy guns, with the silver engraving and the ivory grips: tenderfeet carried those guns. The hardcases didn't care so long as the weapons had good balance and did the killing cleanly.

He holstered his pistol with real satisfaction. "Well, now," he said. "Ain't that shooting? You roll down the bar like that so they can't get a real good sight, and you punch them down with a slug. Pretty slick, huh?"

"You are quite a marksman."

"Say, how come you're so damn palsy-walsy? Usually

I come in and have a good time, and you just stand around and mope, resentin' every glass of your whiskey I get outside of. Today you're all smiles. I never seen you so easy to get along with, MacArdle, and I'd like to know why. You rescuin' one of the soiled doves?"

MacArdle flushed. He swallowed, and his Adam's apple dipped and rose like a badly raised flag. "What?"

"Oh, hell. Don't think I don't know about it. Me and every other man in Virginia City. Least of all, the ones I told, and I sure told everybody who'd listen to me. I heard about how it was for you down at Mother Sue's place the other night. I heard how it was between you and that poor child."

"I just think I might join you," MacArdle said stiffly. He poured himself two fingers of whiskey.

MacArdle's saloon was longer than it was wide, with the solid walnut bar running its length. There were rows of whiskey on shelves on both sides of the bar mirror, which was, for all its importance in MacArdle's eyes, just six feet of ordinary silvered glass.

"Anyway, I have seen and heard a few things in this country," Slade said. "And maybe I've done a few things, so when I come up to old St. Peter, maybe he'll spit in my eye, but I ain't never in my life done anything that ridiculous, MacArdle, and I'm surprised Mother Sue would allow it in a respectable whorehouse. That girl wasn't more than thirteen."

"She was a child. Just a child."

"Well, damn right she was. And you had no right to come in there like any other ordinary miner on a Saturday night and pay Mother Sue the $2 and once you were behind closed doors with that girl to do what you did. I'm thirsty."

MacArdle made a motion toward the bottle, a denying motion. But Slade looked at him until he poured the refill.

"To get behind closed doors with that child under false pretenses. Tsk, tsk, tsk."

"I didn't—"

"No. Of course, you didn't. You didn't do what any normal man would have done. You did somethin' disgraceful, MacArdle, and I tell you, you'll answer for it. Because first off you brought the Good Book into a whorehouse, which, as you surely know, ain't no place for the Book to be. That's somethin' you'll answer for, MacArdle, preachin' to that poor young thing that way."

Something like relief crossed MacArdle's face. His face, which had gotten mottled, smoothed out, and his lungs, which had gotten puffy, wheezed out some air. "That poor child's education had been fearfully neglected."

"And you was just the man to remedy that fault? You know why I like you, MacArdle? You know why I picked you out of all the saloonkeepers in Virginia City to wreck?"

"No, I don't believe so. Why?"

"Because you're such an honest man."

"Thank you."

"I do. I thank you every time I give you my custom."

A figure came in the door, and MacArdle raised his eyes. His eyes were funny: kind of pained, kind of joyous. The customer wasn't who he expected, and his eyes went blank again.

It was Judge Batesworth, perhaps the most important judge in this part of the territory and certainly the most venerable.

"It smells like black powder in here," he remarked. "I don't suppose either of you gentlemen have smelled it." His boots crunched across the floor. "Hello, Mr. Slade. Hello, MacArdle."

"Judge."

"Good to see you, Judge."

Batesworth had served as an officer during Zach Scott's famous charge on the walls of Chapultepec, and he'd been wounded there and awarded the Medal of Honor. Batesworth had fought Indians on the Bozeman Trail and had ridden with Fairweather's original party. The judge was soft-spoken and never carried a gun. He wasn't exactly the chief of all the vigilantes, but the Committee of Vigilance consulted him frequently, and he was the one who had presided over Henry Plummer's brief trial before the necktie party commenced. For some reason, this honorable judge had taken to Jack Slade. Maybe it was his sense of humor. Perhaps it was because both he and Slade were married men. Probably it was Jack Slade's wife.

Slade offered to buy the judge a drink, and the judge accepted graciously and thanked Jack, although no money clattered down on the bar. MacArdle thought that the judge should have thanked him, since it was his whiskey.

Despite Slade's insistence, the judge pulled his glass away when it was only half full. "Just a snort to settle my stomach," he said. He reached into a full bowl of the free lunch enjoyed by any man with the price of a beer. It was roast beef and roast ham and big pickled cucumbers and hard bread from the German bakery. MacArdle was proud of his free lunch. The judge ate a pickle.

"Would have come in for lunch, MacArdle, but my ear heard gunshots, and black powder gives me the gas." He burped, genteelly, of course. He smiled at Jack Slade.

"Didn't always give you the gas, Judge, not when you was giving it to them Mexicans."

"Yes. Well, their food didn't agree with me any better than their politics. MacArdle, you still serve the best drink in Virginia City."

MacArdle didn't know whether to thank the judge. He'd wait and see.

"And how is your wife, Jack?"

"Bonnie's as pretty as ever. My God, I'm lucky to have that woman, Judge. I don't know what I would have become without her."

The judge was quite serious when he said, "The love of a good woman can often redeem a man."

Jack Slade was just as serious when he agreed with him.

"I wish your damn wife could keep you home, out of my saloon," MacArdle said.

"What did you say?" Jack Slade's voice was quite sober, and he was stepping back from the bar where he'd hung out most of the morning when he wasn't shooting holes in MacArdle's property. His hand dangled beside his right hip, about hip high. "I hope you have iron beneath your bar, MacArdle, because I'd sure hate to swing for murder. Excuse me, Judge, for this business, but you heard what he called Bonnie. Now, nobody calls my wife damned, because if she is, it's my business and not anybody else's. Now, you son of a bitch."

"No offense meant. For God's sake, no offense." His hand was in front of his chest, as if he could catch the bullet he expected.

Jack was as suddenly cheerful as he'd been suddenly indignant. "No offense taken," he said with a smile in his voice. "So how you doin', Judge? You still on the right side of the dock?"

The judge smiled very briefly, as if the joke were funny only because Jack Slade had made it. "Jack, I didn't come in here by accident," he said.

"What's on your mind?" Jack cocked his elbow on the bar and twisted to hear every word.

The judge was dead serious. "Jack, you're going to have to change your ways."

"What?"

"Now don't get riled up."

"Riled up? Why the hell should I get riled up? Just because I been talked to like I was no more than knee high and stinking of baby shit."

"Jack, you know me."

"I thought I did." For a second Jack's face was just as sullen as the baby he hated to be called. Then it lit up. "You know that ain't good manners, Judge, you sayin' that sort of thing to me."

"Maybe not. Maybe it isn't my affair, and I should keep upwind of it, but Jack, there have been men talking."

"Talkin' about what?"

"Well, there's been some mention of the Bozeman Trail."

Slade was disgusted. "Judge, you ought to know better than that. You of all men. Me, dressin' myself up as a goddamn Indian and slaughterin' a bunch of innocents. Jesus Christ, you know me better than that."

"I don't believe those rumors. Most of the responsible men discount them."

"Hell, I'm still livin' off what I got sellin' the stage station back to the Overland Company."

"Jack, it isn't what the responsible citizens think that's the problem. You haven't gone out of your way to make friends."

"I got just as many pals as I want. You're one. John Slocum, he's another."

"Two men in five thousand doesn't cast much of a shadow."

"Judge, I do believe you're tryin' to tell me somethin' here. I'd appreciate it if you'd be direct about it and talk to me man to man."

The judge nodded soberly. His eyes sought Jack

Slade's. "The Committee of Vigilance has your name, Jack."

"They what?"

"They are considering your case."

"My case? Now what the hell is that supposed to mean? I'm Jack Slade, married to Bonnie Slade. We got a little shack down out by Green Spring because we don't like livin' too close to all the mud and dust of town. I was born in St. Louis. I never knew my mama or my daddy, either, but I ain't ever backed down from no man in my life. That's what I do, Judge. I don't back down. You put me and the other fellow in the pit, and he'll be hollerin' to get out of that pit long before you ever hear a peep from me. Now, I have thought highly of you, Judge. I've thought highly of your breedin' and the courage you've shown, but, damn, I ain't no case for the Vigilance Committee or anyone else." He threw his whiskey down and slammed his chunky water glass on the bar.

The judge held the angry eyes with his own. "Have you been listening to me, Jack? You know there's only so much your friends can do."

"Do for what? I ain't no damn road agent. The committee's got no business with me."

The judge's eyes left Slade's face and wandered around the saloon until they lighted on MacArdle, where they stayed. "There are those who say otherwise," he said.

Slade missed the significance of the glance. If he'd been just drunk or just mad, he would have caught it, but he was both.

MacArdle backed away down the bar, white as snow. He thought that the judge had just marked him, and he felt the weight of the judge's eyes like a blow.

"You know Bonnie, Judge?"

"Fine woman. None finer," the judge said, not moving his eyes an inch.

"Hell, she'll tell you. She'll tell anyone. I ain't robbed nobody in my life and ain't shot nobody unless he was tryin' to shoot me. MacArdle, you look like a consumptive's last puke. Pour yourself a drink."

MacArdle did as he was bade. He wished that he was out the back door, but he had a fatal attraction to the spot and the accusation that he knew would come right at him.

But the judge in the final analysis was a law and order man, and no lawman worth his salt fails to protect his informants. That's why he gets informants. "I'm sure you're right, Jack," he said, taking his awful gaze off MacArdle. "Thanks for the drink."

"Hey, wait a minute. This ain't settled yet. Not by a long shot."

But Jack was talking to the judge's stiff retreating spine. The judge pushed through the batwings and out into the sunlight.

"What the hell would the committee need with me?" Jack asked. He waved magnanimously. "Have yourself another, MacArdle. And put this damn free lunch away. I ain't hungry now."

MacArdle hurriedly put the free lunch under the bar. When he poured his whiskey, his hands were shaking.

Jack Slade eyed him with a tinge of suspicion in his deep eyes. "Now, what the hell are you so shaky about?" he asked. "Nothin's going to happen." He stopped for a minute. "I've lost all my damn spirit for funnin'. You can start patchin' up Lillie again." He motioned. "Go ahead, man. I ain't going to shoot her again until next time I come."

"I'm out of paste."

"Well, that's too bad. No glue, either, I suppose. Maybe you ought to go over and just get down on your knees and lick that damn painting. Maybe you should pray the damn holes gone. Haw!"

MacArdle hoped that Jack would lose interest, and so he held himself for just a moment, because he was going to have to do any damn awful thing Jack wanted. His best shot was shot.

Jack's mental picture of the owner on his knees licking at the holes in Lillie Langtry faded and was replaced by a dim picture of Bonnie. He backed away from the bar and didn't see MacArdle at all. "Well, partner," he said somewhat vaguely, "I guess I'll be taking my trade down the street, where it'll be appreciated."

Jack Slade turned his back and marched more or less straight toward the batwings with that odd clumsiness of stiff bones and rubber muscles that marks the practiced drunk.

MacArdle leaned back with his eyes closed. The sweat was running out of his forehead as if there would be no end to it, and both his hands were shaking. He got a good whiff of the gunpowder in the air, and he coughed. He gagged. He turned and almost made the back door of the saloon before he started vomiting.

Every man gets used to the blows his life provides, and so Jack Slade tipped his wide-brimmed black hat down over his eyes as he stepped into the bright high-country sunlight. He didn't flinch, although the sudden impact of brightness on his muddied senses was intense. His horse was tied up at the hitch rail, saddle-tight and hangdog. Slade had never bought a good horse in his life, and he didn't make the bad horses he bought any better. Slade eyed him now for his potential to return into MacArdle's and order a drink from that commanding presence. Naw. If he got up on the damn nag's back, he'd get sick, sure as shit. His eyes were squinted against the sun as he tried to make out the figures on the street. It was the usual din after everybody ate lunch and went back to his claim. There was no opposite side of the street, just Alder Gulch, running yellow from sluice to sluice through one claim after another. Jack Slade's eyes happened on the Chinese man who'd bought Slocum's worked-out claim. Slade had had a good laugh over that one. Damn chink would make twice off that claim what Slocum had made. The thought of Slocum's salted claim made him chuckle.

They wouldn't have pulled that stunt on Jack Slade, no sir, because they would have known that he would follow them to the ends of the earth just to shoot them into pieces.

Jack Slade owed his notoriety to the way he'd turned Little Jimmy into dogmeat. The story traveled through a territory that had heard a thing or two and didn't listen to a tale unless it was unusual. Slade rarely thought about that long, booze-soaked afternoon and didn't really remember it. Slade never dreamed, because he always drank himself into bed at night. He didn't remember that day, and he was a little horrified by what he heard he'd done. He thought that killing Jimmy the way it was said he had was a little raw for his usual style.

Somebody said hello.

Slade squinted, squishing his face together so that he looked like a badger. "Who the hell are you?"

"Just a miner. Name of Sheridan, Mr. Slade. Nice day. That's all. Nice day."

"Why you lookin' at me like that? Hell, I don't know you."

"Lookin' at you how, Mr. Slade?" With a touch of toughness, he added, "Just how am I lookin' at you, Mr. Slade?"

That hint was as good as a poster. Slade straightened up, and his face lost its squinty look. He said, "You were lookin' at me like a corpse might look," he said.

That backed the man down. Stumbling over his own

apologies and regrets, the miner hurried up the board-walk, his boots thumping in his haste. Across the gulch, on ground that was certifiably gold-free, silver-free, and value-free, were the rude wooden crosses and plain wooden headboards of Boot Hill. The respectable citizens were buried on the very top of the hill, and the men hanged by the vigilantes had their graves on the near slope, where the headboards tilted and toppled over as Alder Creek undercut the cemetery. The grass on Boot Hill was rank and green, much greener than grass anywhere else in Virginia City. The unnatural, too-rich greenery gave Slade the creeps.

He never thought about the men he had killed. Once dead, they were his past, a record of his achievements, which, if not eternal as stone, surely were permanent.

It was hot, and he was already starting to sweat. Trouble with the damn booze is that it soaked right through him and stained every shirt he owned until he could hardly wear them. Bonnie cut his destroyed shirts apart and restitched them, because the cash from the stage-station sale was going pretty fast; once it was gone, he'd have to hire on again.

He never did like to work for other men. He hated to have anybody tell him how to spend his time. He never thought that his time was an infinite resource, and he hated to waste it taking orders. He grinned at himself. He was thinking so seriously, worse than that damn MacArdle, reading the Bible to a little whore girl.

The girl had come downstairs with MacArdle in tow, crying all over her face. "Get this bastard out of here," she had said, and MacArdle was barred forever from saving the souls of poor doves at Mother Sue's.

Damn, he was lucky to have Bonnie, best thing that had ever happened to him. He sat down on the front stoop of "VIRGINIA CITY GENERAL MERCH." with his back against the big window where they had the new black iron pans and the pick heads and shovel blades and the variety of handles. New equipment made mining look like a shiny business rather than the grueling, monotonous work it really was.

At least he had some shade, and under the wide brim of his hat his eyes were cool and rested. He really shouldn't do this. The damn judge was right. He really had to change his way of living. Two women came down the boardwalk until they were about twenty feet away from his outstretched legs before they went into the street to pass by him.

He tipped his hat politely. "Ma'am. Ma'am."

One woman sniffed. The other didn't see him any better than she would have seen a bug or a pile of dog scat. He grinned at them all the same. He knew what they apparently didn't know. He was no damn bachelor; he was a married man and faithful to one woman: Bonnie.

"Beautiful Bonnie," he said aloud.

He heard something behind him and cranked himself around to watch one of the mercantile clerks staring at him. The clerk retreated, half scared, and Slade wondered what had scared him so much.

Beautiful Bonnie. Bonnie was the third wife of a jack Mormon down near Provo the first time Jack Slade saw her. It was a nice station. As a professional, Slade had to give them that: The Mormons knew how to keep a nice stage station. They'd put it up near a good spring in the mouth of a ravine where about half the day you had shade. And they didn't water their livestock right in the spring; they constructed a runoff trough and fenced the spring so that it didn't get foul with droppings. The station was set back under some junipers that would break the wind in wintertime and shade the house in summer. The house was adobe and wood.

Jack rode into the station one afternoon, and he got a

glimpse of Bonnie as she hurried out of sight. Those Mormons didn't care too much for outsiders glimpsin' their wives, and from what he'd just seen, Jack Slade couldn't blame them. Bonnie had hair that was honey blond, not the pale honey that comes in the spring, but the richer auburn honey—thistle honey in the fall. She was a tall woman, and she ran like she'd used her muscles. Even under the all-purpose covering of her dress, Jack Slade could guess at her breasts. He forgot about it when he met her husband, because Jack wanted to trade horses. She served him his dinner that night because both Jack and the Mormon were stubborn traders and there was too much at stake to be hasty.

The Mormon didn't introduce the woman who brought their dinner, bowl after steaming bowl, and she kept her eyes downcast. God, she was handsome. Once again Jack Slade forgot about the whole thing, and the next morning he rode away from the station, without his horses but with some gold coin. Two miles out, she waited beside the trail for him, and when he passed, she rode alongside. Although he was pretty damn curious to know what a woman was doing out there in the middle of Indian country, he never asked. He figured that it was her business to tell him if she wanted to, and otherwise, well, he wasn't a blabby man himself. She had blue eyes that were bird-sharp and fairly active, much more active than his. She was always squirming around on her sidesaddle, eyeballing this, looking at that, as if the world were a constant wonder to her. Later, when he got to know her better, he suspected that it actually was.

He wonder where Slocum was now. Maybe he should look up his old buddy and lift a drink. It was comfortable sitting in the shade, and if he was blocking the mercantile's doorway, well, all anybody had to do was ask. He'd move. He wasn't nearly so rude as people supposed.

It was good in the sun, and Jack Slade was remembering. He'd been sober that day, been sober for a week before he hit the station up in the damn San Christos, mustanging. Of course, the jack Mormon didn't offer him a drink, although Slade was sure that the bastard had a bottle or two around someplace.

She rode well. From time to time she hummed something. It was monotonous and soft and might have been a lullaby. That night they camped at a little Indian seep Slade knew. He had intended to camp along the Colorado, where there was an abundance of water and a good supply of dry cottonwood, but he made a hard camp instead, a good hour off the trail, because he knew that the Mormons didn't take kindly to their wives riding off with other men, willing or not. Slade had heard tales about Mormon gunmen—"Death's Angels" they called them—and what he had heard made the vigilantes look like a bunch of tenderfeet. The vigilantes just hanged you. When the Death's Angels got to the rope part, most men were glad to have it over with.

He'd built a modest fire and put on his old, trail-blackened coffee pot. She gathered firewood quietly. From a small pack on the back of her own horse, she withdrew a small iron pot, which she filled at the seep, and then she heated water. When the water was warm, she washed her hands and face. Still sitting, she unbuttoned her dress at the neck. She wore no petticoats or camisole or chemise, which was not what he'd heard about Mormon women. She washed the tops of her taut breasts and then the undersides, dabbing at them with her washcloth. He shifted his seat beside the fire as she undid her hair and shook it out. Her eyes were not on his, but they were all she concealed. She unbuttoned herself, opened her dress wide, and washed her flat belly and her strong thighs and her bush, too. She stood and cast her dress off and faced him finally with her eyes.

"My name's Bonnie, Mr. Slade," she said. "And I aim to change my luck."

She did, both that night and plenty of other nights after that. They got married in Denver because he wanted to. She was indifferent to the benefits of marital bliss and laughingly reminded him that the marriage was illegal since she hadn't bothered to get unmarried from her previous husband. Otherwise, she never spoke about her previous husband.

Bonnie Slade was the only decent thing that had ever happened to him, and he was grateful for it. He would be until the day he died.

He opened his eyes because somebody was standing in his sunlight. Trousers, many men wearing trousers. Miner's trousers and grocer's trousers and the pinstriped trousers that were fashionable with the tinhorns.

X. Beidler blocked his sunlight.

"Jack," the German said, "we have come for you."

3

"Will you look at that." The Yellow Kid was alone at the door, watching. Slocum didn't care to look, didn't want to be bothered with whatever was outside. He was eating.

When wolves finally bring down an elk after a long hungry time, for a moment the blood gushes and the entrails steam, and that moment is perhaps the only time when buck wolves feel community. For a moment there is enough for everybody: enough for the strongest, the weakest, the newest, and the past-his-prime. No snapping then, no nipping or threats. It was community pure and simple.

The Irish miner wore a grin as big as the territory across his face, but it was pretty sickly, as if he'd been caught out at something. In the past hour, he'd lost better than a pound of gold, the bulk of it to John Slocum.

Although Slocum was a skillful gambler, he couldn't attribute this victory to skill. The miner was determined to throw it away, and Slocum had the biggest hat to catch what fell, which is another way of saying that he had the cards. If the Irishman drew to a straight and hit, Slocum was holding a flush. The Irishman's two pair didn't look so good against Slocum's trips. The largest pot of the afternoon was a mound of yellow gold that threatened to spill over the scale pan. There must have been eight ounces of it, and the miner wouldn't back down. He had three queens, and Slocum was showing nothing but fours and sevens, two of each. Stubbornly, the miner held on. He was feeling flush and was thinking that maybe he wouldn't have to hit the trail, after all, that maybe this one pot would be enough to keep him in Virginia City for a spell.

The tinhorn and his partner had folded long ago. They were content to let Slocum have the big pots, although they did flash their teeth when he won big with a king high or a low pair. Of course, Slocum did have the third seven, which wasn't enough to beat three queens unless you counted in the pair of fours that made it a full house. The Irishman's face fell. He mumbled something about the mother lode.

"I heard it was up above Nevada Gulch," the tinhorn said helpfully.

"You knucklehead. If it was above Nevada Gulch, what would keep the men in Nevada Gulch from finding it?" The miner's sneer was exaggerated, and everybody knew that he had a good idea where to search for the mother lode, a place that appealed to all his practical knowledge and his belief in magical qualities as well.

When these prospectors talked about a place they meant to search, once the talk passed beyond words like "reef gold" and "telluride" and "overthrusts" and "quartzite," they'd sigh and say something like, "And Harry, it's such a lovely place for gold." Slocum had heard them talking this way, working themselves up.

Slocum thought about reminding the miner to save some dust in case the mother lode wasn't there, but he said nothing. Like the miner, he was a man who went all the way. Root hog or die. He never saw any sense in trying a thing with anything held back in reserve in case it failed. If a man wanted to give his best, he had to give all of it, not eighty percent or ninety percent. Slocum was philosophizing because the mound of gold had been emptied into his poke, and the miner who hadn't expected that full house was playing for openers now.

Which was when the Yellow Kid exclaimed at the doorway.

"Bring us another jug of pot liquor," the tinhorn called.

"Get it yourself," the Yellow Kid said. He went behind the bar and put his coat on and was straightening his string tie in the mirror. "It's jump or slide out there, boys, and I aim to see the end of it."

The tinhorn put down his cards. "The committee?"

"Sure looks like it. Must be two or three hundred men, and there's one out front with a rope swingin' from his paw. Have a nice game." He put the cashbox in the open safe and, after a moment, the two surviving bottles of the owner's private stock. He slammed the safe door and spun the dials.

He was busting through the door, and his words came back to the card players brokenly, "Jack . . . Slade. . . ."

Slocum's ears pricked up. "Slade?"

The tinhorn yawned. "That's what he said."

John Slocum tugged the drawstring of his poke shut. "Much as I hate to walk out of a game when I'm ahead. . . ."

The miner looked up and whined. He'd been waiting for a good chance to whine since he had sat down at the game, and now he had it. "You mean you're not going to give me a chance to win back my dust?"

"Oh, hell," Slocum said. "Oh, hell. The hell with you. You piss it away to somebody else now. I'm sure these gents would be happy to oblige you."

The tinhorn smiled happily, with little teeth that

glistened like the teeth of something that gets a good hold and won't let go.

Now that Slocum's attention was free, he could hear the murmur and the shouts and the calls from the boardwalk outside the Bullwhacker.

Slocum had been out to Slade's soddy twice before, which was twice more than any other man in Virginia City. Slade spent a good bit of time out there because of Bonnie. For a man who liked fast living, it had no other outstanding attractions.

Slocum's visits hadn't been altogether comfortable. Slade never drank at home, and Slocum felt obliged to avoid drinking, too, because he didn't want to make it hard on his host.

The soddy had two rooms, and the one Slocum had been invited into was extremely neat. It was a combination kitchen, dining room, and living room: one big room across the house, with three windows and a door that opened onto a spacious front porch. The back of the soddy was built into a hill, and the front walls were thick enough and pounded well to stop an Indian arrow or a bullet.

An Indian rug of Navajo design lay on the dirt floor. The other furniture had obviously been made by Slade himself. A couple of wide flat boards were spiked through the end grain to make a not particularly sturdy table. A piece of joshua wood made an armchair if you didn't mind sitting in the fork of a tree with one branch sawed off just beyond your elbow. The other chairs were benches constructed in the same manner as the table. There were a couple of kerosene lamps and the cookstove, a Pickoak. The shelves on the walls, used for storage, looked homemade, and Jack Slade offered Slocum the joshua tree, remarking proudly, "Now I ain't no cabinetmaker."

"You bet."

"But me and Bonnie, we ain't fancy folks. Not fancy folks at all." Slade put one arm around his wife to demonstrate affection and ownership. Bonnie wouldn't look Slocum in the eye.

Slocum sat on the tree, and it was slightly less comfortable than it looked. "Uh-huh."

Remembering his duties, Slade offered Slocum coffee or fresh water or tea. He explained that Bonnie wouldn't let him drink at home.

Bonnie Slade didn't look so tough to Slocum. She was a slightly fleshy woman with good hips and fine high breasts. A wisp of dark blond hair was hanging down into her face, and occasionally she'd sweep it back with a quick nervous motion.

The nearest whites were three miles to the south at a place called Stinking Springs. Slocum said that it must get lonely out here when Jack was in town.

"You sayin' I'm gone away too long?" Jack took a step toward him, and John Slocum wished that he wasn't dangled across the joshua tree. If it came to a fight, he wouldn't be able to do a thing.

Slocum said something about no offense. Slade clenched his hands hard so that his fingertips turned white, and said, "Heh-heh." There was no offense taken.

"There'll be no violence in my house," Bonnie Slade said to nobody in particular.

Jack Slade hung his head. "No, Bonnie," he said. And he added, "I'm sorry."

An apology from Jack Slade was slightly less common than hen's teeth, and Slocum's eyebrows rose in surprise.

"I keep a good house, Mr. Slocum," Bonnie Slade said. "My home is neat, and I cook Jack a good meal when he comes home. When he's away, I bar the door at night and keep a scattergun leaning against the sill, day and night. If an Indian or a white man should care to take advantage of a lone woman in an isolated house, they shall be disappointed here."

"You have an unusual way of speaking," Slocum said.

"What'd you mean by that?" Slade's fist clenched again. Slocum got out of the chair and stood against the far wall of the soddy, with his heel holding him off the wall. "I meant that Mrs. Slade talks like an educated person, like an officer or a lawyer."

Slade's fists unclenched again, and the smile that spread across his pan was wonderful. "Yeah," he said. "That's what I say myself." He gave his wife a buffet across the bottom that was hard enough to lift her a few inches, which she ignored.

"I believe a woman can make opportunities just as a man can," Bonnie said rather primly.

The next time he came out, John Slocum brought her a couple books he'd bought from a thespian turned gold miner. He brought her a copy of Shakespeare's *As You Like It* and a collection of essays by Ralph Waldo Emerson. Slocum wasn't a reader, but a couple of men who were had said that they were both good books.

Those books almost got Slocum killed. Jack Slade was more than ordinarily jealous, and the smile of pure pleasure that went over his wife's face sent a stab to his heart. Bonnie Slade was rarely flustered. Jack Slade once watched her cut a nine-foot timber rattler in half with a hoe as if it were as exciting as sweeping the porch. But these books thrilled her, and she blushed like a girl. John Slocum felt danger. He was formally polite and called her "ma'am" and explained that he'd intended the books as a gift to the entire Slade household. Jack Slade couldn't read or write a word and said so right away, challenging Slocum's right to give his wife anything that would please her more than the bunch of wild flowers he'd picked on the trail out from Virginia City, which now reposed in a tin can on the table he'd built with his own hands.

"I know you can't read, Jack," Slocum said. "Maybe your wife might take the time to teach you."

"Can't teach an old dog new tricks," Slade said sourly.

"It's a fine gift, Mr. Slocum. A fine gift. One who likes reading can't be long satisfied with reading the labels on canned goods. I mean to be an educated woman someday. I mean to improve myself." She got flustered then because she'd let too much of her real self slip through her reserve. She went straight to the stove, where she poured them each a cup of hot coffee that neither man wanted.

Tin cup in hand, Jack Slade paced back and forth. He was restless. Slocum wasn't much more comfortable than during his previous visit. He'd had some strange idea that it might be nice to be inside a real household again, but this one was less pleasing to him than a saloon or a whorehouse. He stepped outside and sat on the porch, and a moment later Slade joined him. Both men held the steaming cups in their hands, and both were uncomfortable. They could be pals on opposite sides of a poker table or leaning against a bar, but out here? They didn't have a daylight relationship.

Slade jerked his finger back toward the quiet house. "I ain't never seen her smile like that," he said.

"It was just a little thing."

"Not to her it wasn't."

They drank their coffee, and Slocum thought of some excuse for riding out of Jack Slade's love nest and never coming back again.

Instead, Mrs. Slade came into town. She got the two books in October, and there was deep December snow on the trails when Slocum saw her again. She was dressed in a cast-off sheepskin of Jack's, and her fine honey hair was completely hidden in a thick wool scarf, as she went into the office of Judge Batesworth right there on Main Street.

Like most of the law setups in town, the judge's office was just one room facing the street, right beside the barbershop, which was somewhat better than being next to a saloon or gambling hall, since barbers are quieter.

"Something I can do for you, miss?"

Bonnie Slade removed her heavy scarf and shook the snow off it before she stepped toward the old judge with her hand extended like a man. "I am Bonnie Slade, Judge. And I understand from my husband Jack that you are the best-educated man in Virginia City and perhaps in the territory."

That surprised the judge. He had been working. He put his pen into its holder and demurred politely. "I have some education, ma'am, but there are many better-educated men than me."

She set the two books, Slocum's gift, on the judge's desk. She had wrapped them in oilskin, and they were in good condition. "I am anxious to improve my education. I have a proposition. I would like you to select books for me from your own library. Two at a time. I will exchange them for these books. You will never be out, even if some awful accident happens to the two books I have."

"Now wait a minute, young lady."

"Will you help me?"

"Of course, I'll help you. Of course, I will."

The upshot was that Bonnie Slade came under the personal tutelage of the judge. Every week they had lessons in his office. Since this office was on the ground floor facing the gulch and anybody could look inside, there never was any suspicion of any hanky-panky going on—particularly since Jack Slade sat on the curb outside during the lesson and, as soon as it was over, hurried his wife home again.

Virginia City was full of good people who admired self-improvement, and most of them practiced it in some form or another—usually the improvement of their pokes. Most of them had expected Jack Slade's wife to be a slattern, a fat, blowsy, hard-mouthed whore. To find an attractive, modest woman—scarcely more than a girl —who took lessons from the most prominent man in town came as a real surprise. Mrs. Jack Slade soon moved up in folks' estimation, and Jack Slade moved up, too, because of the woman he'd married.

Now they were going to hang Jack.

Slocum's Appaloosa stretched out. Its fine rambunctious freshness had worn off, and now it was in the groove and could run all day.

The Appaloosa jumped two prospect holes crossing the sagebrush plain, but Slocum's luck held, and he hadn't hit any mine shafts or holes too broad to jump. He was able to shave some time.

If he could get Bonnie Slade and get back in time . . . .

The familiar soddy grew bigger as he booted the Appaloosa home. He was feeling better than he should. The ride was clearing the poker fumes from his mind, and he had nearly a pound of gold dust tied to the saddle ring under his knee, which was more money than he'd seen in a while.

Jack Slade wasn't kin. Jack Slade wasn't even that good a friend.

His horse kicked up dirt clods galloping into Slade's front yard. The door was pulled closed, and a shotgun barrel was fixed on his middle. That was how she greeted all her visitors, and she didn't put it away once she recognized him. She stepped out the door with the shotgun in one hand and a book in the other. "Why, Mr. Slocum."

"Ma'am, Jack's in bad trouble. I think you'd better come with me into town."

"What sort of trouble?" she asked pleasantly, without letting go of the shotgun or losing her place.

"The Vigilance Committee has him."

"Yes?"

"Bonnie, they're going to hang him high as a kite unless you get into town and ask them real sweet not to."

"Oh." Her face lost some color, and the book dropped from her hand. She thought fast and hard. "Yes," she said. "I expect that comes under our agreement."

That puzzled Slocum, but time was wasting.

She had a horse tied out in back. Once she started moving, she didn't waste a motion. He came down to help her saddle up, but she had the blanket on her horse's back and the saddle up and the cinch buckle on and booted tight before he could lift a hand. She flung her bridle across the horse's nose, and Slocum noted the heavy spade bit that could ruin a horse's mouth in the hands of a rough rider.

"Ho!" she shouted, and took off ahead of him, riding astride, just like a man, with her honey hair streaming out behind her.

Bonnie Slade kept her promises. There were those who cursed her, called her harlot, adultress, and worse, but none of her enemies denied that she was a woman of her word, through and through.

Women usually are better with the spirit of the law than its letter, the observance of which seems more a man's habit.

She'd been born near Provo to a family of English Mormons. Her family had been recruited by missionaries. The Newcastle collieries were closing; there was cheaper coal in Cardiff, coal that was easier to mine and took fewer hands. Massive unemployment always effects religious conversion, and Bonnie's parents were eager to hear of a land across the sea called Zion where good work and good morals would produce happiness and prosperity.

The boat wasn't all that it should have been. Between its crowded decks, disease raged, and many of the passengers died. The wagon train from St. Louis, which many dreaded, was actually much easier. They crossed the deserts in the cool of the spring, when there was plenty of water and nights were good for sleeping. They didn't see a single unfriendly redskin, although they never got careless on that account. Four hundred wagons of European converts: Danes and Swedes and Englishmen and Scots, a few Germans and Swiss. They were led by the church's own guides, men who'd taken a dozen such trains across hostile country to Zion.

In the 1840s, when Bonnie was born, the territory of Utah, under Brigham Young, was the closest thing to a nation within a nation that America has ever seen. Utah Territory was a theocracy guided by divine guidance as interpreted by the church elders.

They had started the immense wooden tabernacle in Salt Lake City. They were an industrious people who took the bee as their symbol and put the beehive on all their currency and official documents. The Mormons made peace with the Indians, converting the Piutes to white men's ways. Mormon missionaries, called farmers by the church, lived with the tribes like resident Indian agents.

They were a forthright people. Soon the desert bloomed under their plows, and irrigation systems brought water down from the snowline to valleys that hadn't known water since creation.

They were a strict people. When Bonnie was ten, her mother fell in love with another man and went off with him. She was ostracized. Her husband, a mild-mannered man, was told in no uncertain words what to do to bring his erring spouse back into line.

They fought. His killing her was more or less accidental, but he was hanged.

Bonnie's new family contained three wives and a corpulent elder of the church, a feed merchant named Jebediah Tull. Jebediah had the girl's virginity when she was fifteen. The church might have protected her if it had been known, but she never told, and Jebediah certainly didn't.

Once a week after that time, Jebediah used her like he used his other wives, penetrating her while she was dry, puffing away on top of her while he mauled her breasts with both hands. When he climaxed, he left her bed. With his other wives, he stayed all night, but Jebediah was nothing if not discreet.

Bonnie watched and waited. Steadily she grew more beautiful. When she was seventeen, another man, a certain Johnson who owned a stage station in the mountains, started looking at her in the temple on the sabbath. On the days he was in town, he'd make excuses to stop and chat. He wasn't a bad man, apparently kind, and his other wives hadn't had the spirit knocked out of them. They laughed and told jokes in a way that the stricter Mormons thought just shy of scandalous. Bonnie took it as a good sign.

Johnson's appearance was a bad sign. He had a weak chin. What he'd lost in the chin, he'd gained in his Adam's apple. He had a ready smile, but his cheeks were so sharp that you could see only one side of his smile at a time.

In those days the church was having trouble. All those legislators back in Washington envisioned a Sodom and Gomorrah in Utah Territory. The image of busy little bees didn't mean much to them.

Utah was a special place. To the east of it was desert,

mountains, and Indians. To the west were mountains, deserts, and Indians. The immigrant trains that forged their way through one set of hazards found Utah and the lush irrigated valleys to be a land of milk and honey. And if Mormon traders drove too sharp a bargain for their wheel rims and horseshoes, extra powder and lead, that was nothing to be surprised at—they had the only goods in a thousand miles.

The government sent parties west to investigate the so-called Kingdom of Deseret. The Mormons suspected, with good reason, that those parties of Army surveyors were in fact spies.

The survey parties met with accidents and Indians.

The federal government talked about war, and probably if Brigham Young hadn't sent a battalion of volunteers to save California for the Union, there would have been war.

Friendly legislators in Washington sent the Mormons the word: No more multiple marriages.

Nobody liked that. Polygamy worked to the benefit of women, because they could parcel out the hardships. In the normal course of frontier life, a man outlived three or four wives, but when three or four wives spread the load, everybody kept busy and nobody died of overwork. In the tremendous isolation, the women provided company for one another.

The men spoke about God's law, and they enjoyed variety, which a fortuitous divine law prescribed.

Bonnie didn't care, because she was out of her adoptive father's house and away from his heavy body and under a new man who was kinder, uglier, and much lighter. He liked to kiss her a lot at first, explaining that he often kissed his other wives, but Bonnie felt uncomfortable with the kissing in a way that sex itself didn't make her uncomfortable.

While she was living with her husband, she saw Jack

Slade. At first she didn't see the real Jack Slade. Her Jack Slade was sober, an uncommon situation that Bonnie took to be the ordinary run of events. The sight of him—the first non-Mormon male she'd ever seen up close—sent Bonnie's young heart to puzzling. She went back to the room the wives shared and worked on her needlework, but she wasn't thinking about needlework as her fingers flew.

Bonnie sat up after the others went to bed and thought about her life. She found the thinking very exciting. Her fingers did their work, and her mind did its work. She saw how it would be if she stayed, how she would become a mother to first one and then more children, until she was no longer able to conceive. She would stretch and groan, and the marks of aging would come upon her. When she tied off one corner of her needlework, she said, "Goodness," because her nimble fingers had constructed a pyramid of knots. She giggled too softly for the other wives to hear.

She didn't mind being married, didn't mind Mr. Johnson's perfunctory lovemaking, and didn't mind getting old and lined. How could she? But the idea of living a life where she hadn't seen anything at all didn't appeal to her. Once again her fingers flew, disassembling the knots she'd just finished. This time it was no automatic job, nothing routine. She picked at each nasty little knot until she could get her hook through it and tug it loose.

She thought that she would have to become a new person. She wasn't so very naive; in fact, she didn't have a naive bone in her body. Leaving the station would be dangerous, and her protection would be less than it had been. She worried at one knot with her fine sharp teeth. "Darn."

She thought, Well, we protect livestock, too, the cows

and the horses, but they don't have any more freedom than I do.

She looked at her sleeping friends, the two women she'd sewed with, sat up with, and worried with. When one was blue, the other two commiserated; when one was sick, the others shouldered her part of the load. She'd miss the other wives more than Johnson.

She put down her needlework. It was half finished, just like her life. Silently she stole around the bedroom, gathering her few possessions: the tortoise-shell comb she'd had from her mother, one locket, and a clean dress. She took the second-best horse on the place, figuring that she'd surely done enough work to earn it. She took no provisions. She meant to trade one man for another, to use her body for her protection.

Although Jack Slade had been with plenty of women, they'd all been whores, and so he was better at joking with women than touching them. He was no better as a lover that first night under the bright stars than the two men who had preceded him in Bonnie's life. He meant to get on, get in, and get off, but he was a little spooked by her sudden appearance, and he was cold sober and had started to dry out a little. He took more time than he had intended getting on her and more time getting in.

Perhaps it was the excitement of what she was doing, the sheer thrill of the novelty or the wickedness, but under him, Bonnie began to feel like she'd never felt before, like she was not supposed to feel. She felt a warmth in her groin and a slow languorous warmth spreading through the small of her back. Soon her hips were moving of their own accord in a way she might have thought lewd and lascivious if she'd been capable of thinking just then, which she certainly was not.

"Oh," she said. Then she said, "Oh, please. Please."

Jack Slade was more familiar with the female orgasm in the breach than in the observance, but he knew enough to know what he had. The young girl was rolling under him, and so he slowed down a little to let her catch up with him.

She did.

Afterward, lying close together under that blazing heaven, Bonnie thought that there would be a new life, and it would be marvelous. She didn't love this stranger —the man who'd given her so much pleasure—but she felt that she could, given half a chance.

Trust Jack Slade not to give it to her. When she waited for him in their room in the fanciest hotel in Denver with the bucket of champagne and the new nightgown she'd bought on the advice of one of Denver's fancy ladies, an old friend of Jack's, while she was waiting, he was off having a party of his own. He was drinking himself stupid at his own wedding party, turning a one-night celebration into a week-long affair.

That did it. Bonnie lay under Jack Slade after that while he puffed and grunted. Sometimes she liked him and sometimes not, but she never reached the same ecstasy she'd enjoyed the first night they met. She found it hard to make women friends, perhaps because she'd lived so closely with women for such a long time that casual acquaintances didn't seem quite real to her. She never found out that orgasms were not so awfully rare as she thought.

In time she learned all about Jack Slade—the ferocity of his enmities and the snarls of the men who hated him. She was fiercely loyal. Jack Slade hadn't done so very much for Bonnie, merely riding her out of Utah when that was the direction he was intending to go, anyway. Jack Slade couldn't go back into Deseret, and as a man of good sense, he gave Idaho a miss, too, because the Mormons had put the word on him, accused him of kidnaping a good woman and turning her from the ways of the Lord, and that was, God knows, a hanging offense. Jack didn't care whether he did business in Utah or Idaho, anyway. It was no skin off his nose.

Bonnie's loyalty had to fix on something or someone. Once in Cheyenne, one of Jack's enemies (Little Jimmy Eads's cousin) planned to murder him after he passed out drunk. Bonnie took the shotgun and hurried into a saloon that hadn't seen a married woman in quite some time. Jack was passed out in the corner, and Bonnie patrolled that corner with the shotgun in her hands, daring anybody to come and get her Jack. There were a few men in that room who might have slaughtered a woman, but none was bold enough to do it publicly. Besides, the shotgun had barrels big enough to garage a coach and four, and maybe she'd get lucky.

He loved her, and she didn't love him, but she felt a strong gratitude to the man who'd set her free and given her pleasure for the first time in her life. When she liked Denver, she slept with Slade. When she got excited by the bustle and flurry in Last Chance Gulch, she took him home and put her mouth on his cock, which she'd never done in her life and he'd never had done by any woman he hadn't paid. She was disappointed when he came into her mouth because she always hoped to come again with him inside of her. But it wasn't to be. Jack Slade thought that one round was the whole fight and dozed off, leaving his unsatisfied wife on the bed beside him.

They had rules. He didn't approach her unless he was sober, which, as his drinking got worse, meant that the lovemaking got rare. He wasn't supposed to drink at their home. If their home was a hotel room or a shanty, it made no difference—no booze was allowed. He was allowed to bring his friends home, but only if everybody stayed sober. Once, in Deadwood, she'd been pinched by one of Jack's drinking buddies, and she vowed to have no repeats of that performance. She stayed home and took care of his house. When he was home, she fed him, talked to him, and did his laundry. More and more lately he stayed away, raising hell. Their money was running low, and Bonnie was concerned, because she thought that Jack would go on the outlaw trail once his last dime was gone, and she surely wouldn't follow him there. Her loyalty had some limits.

Although she didn't know it, Jack Slade treated her like he'd treated no other woman in his life. In his own way, he loved her more than he loved life. Jack Slade would have died for her, but that wouldn't have made her love him any more. That was the sad thing about it.

She'd learned to read because literacy wasn't as uncommon among the Mormon women as it was in the rest of the country. She'd read the Book of Mormon, the *Deseret News*, and, as she said, every tin can label that passed through the house. Slocum's casual gift of the two books brought her wealth like she'd never imagined. It wasn't the ownership of the books that thrilled her, it was the reading of them that gave her a joy she'd never known before.

What the books did was direct and powerful. They moved her into the second room of her new freedom. Like the hotel in Denver and the hurly-burly of the crowds in Last Chance Gulch, the books showed her more of life, but they showed her more than that. They showed her that life was rich and variable, that there was room in it for more than one way of looking at things and more than one way of living. That was the lesson she learned and the lesson that powered her out of the shanty and into Virginia City to get an education. She needed to find out what she could be; that was what Bonnie Slade needed.

Now John Slocum was at the soddy, and Jack Slade was in trouble again: the man who had given her freedom, the drunk, the manslayer, her husband. She hesitated and then hurried around the back of her house and saddled her fast horse. That was her agreement; that was the price she paid.

4

"Oh, climb down," Jack Slade said, flushing red. "Ain't no bunch of hardheads going to buffalo me." He looked away and spat on the sidewalk. It wasn't quite the performance he'd hoped for, since tobacco juice stained the corner of his lip. He stared at the splotch on the boardwalk. One muddy splotch on a muddy wooden boardwalk. He wondered how long the boardwalk would last before it was torn up and burned for firewood. He wiped his mouth angrily. No sense thinking that way; no good could come of it.

"We ain't here to buffalo you, Jack." Beidler smiled. His smile was one of the most awful things Jack Slade had ever seen. It reminded him of Little Jimmy Eads's smile once the sun started stretching out his face.

"Jack, you're a dangerous man."

For the first time in his life, Jack Slade looked at X. Beidler, really looked at him. X. Beidler was short and stout, not much higher than the hollow in Jack Slade's neck. (No, it was not a good idea to think about the subject of necks, Jack told himself.) He must have weighed nearly two hundred. It wasn't hard muscle, and it wasn't sloppy fat, either. X. Beidler wore his prosperity around his body like another suit of clothes. His suit was dark, blue or black; it was too dusty to tell. He wore

a greasy bowler hat tilted onto the back of his head. His
hair was fair, what there was of it, and his little blue eyes
had a glint of genuine humor. If Jack Slade could come
up with a better joke than his own death, X. Beidler
would have to let him alone.

Jack was more angry than alarmed, and he stopped the
whole crowd of vigilantes on the narrow boardwalk.
They were starting to spread out onto the street now, like
a leakage. Jack didn't like that much, because they were
bound to surround him, but that couldn't be helped.
Sometimes a man lost all his authority objecting to a
matter of principle that doesn't matter much.

Jack had done nothing. He knew that, and the crowd
knew it. Nothing could be proved against Jack Slade.
The lengthy target practice on Little Jimmy Eads was
known to be horrible, but since Slade had been acting in
defense of property—the stagecoach station at the
Springs and the property thereon, property belonging to
the Overland Stage Company, Inc.—nobody ever complained much about it. Jack had never spoken about the
other men he'd killed. Drunk or sober, he knew how to
hold his tongue.

He put his hands on his hips, leaned back, and looked
at the heavens. Maybe somebody up there was witness-
ing this comedy, and he was playing to the expensive
seats. "Ha, ha," he said. "Ha. God damn, Beidler. Get
out of my way or I'll get angrier than I like to be."

Beidler smiled, but he didn't say a word.

The sun was bright, and the sky overhead was a distant
cold blue. In the west a "V" of Canada geese was
honking its way south, the first of the season. They were
so high, Slade couldn't hear their calls. Maybe if all
these men weren't breathing around him, he could hear
the geese. Jack Slade thought that it would be just
wonderful if all these men who, after all, had nothing
against one another could sit down on the boardwalk and

watch the passage of the geese overhead. He meant to say something about it, but one look at Beidler's smile chased the notion out of his head. He swallowed. It tasted like he'd swallowed all the possibilities of peace and harmony, and the anger rose in him, bitter and hot as bile.

"Beidler, you're a dead man," he said. He dropped his hands to his sides and spread his feet apart for a better stance. Men on both sides of the dusty German moved aside. Because of the crowd, movement was difficult; those who could, stepped into the streets. A lane formed behind X. Beidler, wide enough to let bullets penetrate his body without penetrating others.

Still Beidler smiled. His smile reminded Slade of the smiles he'd seen on the religious statues favored by Catholic miners. "Sir?" Beidler inquired politely.

Slade jabbed his thumb at his own chest. His face was contorted with wrath, and he jabbed himself again for emphasis. "You ain't going to murder me," he snarled.

"Oh hell, Jack. No thought of murdering you. No, indeed. We just thought we'd straighten out some of your wanton ways."

Again Jack Slade spat. This time he didn't have a bit of juice for it. When he rubbed the corner of his mouth, it was dry. "I ain't no damn road agent, and you know it," he said.

"Well," Beidler said pleasantly, "you ain't exactly a exemplary citizen either. If you was to advertise as a citizen, wouldn't be too many communities would be takers."

Slade looked at him.

"No, not many." Beidler sounded damned smug.

"Oh, to hell with you. To hell with you." To Jack Slade's ears, his words sounded weak and tentative, and he knew that words could put that noose around his neck as surely as men's hands could. He raised his voice so that all the men in the back could hear him. "Any men in this necktie party? One man? One man who'll dare speak to me? You there, Yellow Kid. I see you tryin' to slip behind that big galoot. What the hell you doin' out here?"

The Yellow Kid said something, but Slade couldn't hear him because of a roaring in his ears.

"What did you say? Louder, Kid. How come you're out here in the street in broad daylight to murder me? Never thought you was that sort, Kid. Thought you and me was pards."

Once more the words had betrayed poor Jack. Just as he was making headway with them, they turned around, thickened in his mouth, and did him more harm than good. The Yellow Kid didn't want to be known as Jack Slade's partner. Not here and not now. If Jack had stopped before his question, probably the Kid would have mumbled something like, "Nothing personal. Nothing personal against you, Jack" and would have made himself as small as he could, retired behind some bigger men, and probably left the crowd. Probably a few more would have followed him, because after all, hanging a man was exciting, but it didn't get any mining done. The weather was going to be turning cold, and Alder Gulch would freeze solid, and then nobody would make any money. But the Yellow Kid wasn't any partner of Jack Slade's, not today.

He blurted out, "I never saw you before in my goddamn life."

That was as large a lie as that crowd had heard in many days, and it brought out a deep, rumbling kind of laugh. The crowd knew just why the Yellow Kid was trying to put distance between himself and Jack Slade.

The laugh brought the Yellow Kid partway back to his senses. He'd slipped in behind a couple of miners and peeked out, shy as a baby bird. Then he opened his mouth to say, "That man Slocum. He's the only damn friend you got."

Somebody said, "Where's Slocum?"

Somebody else took up the call. The words ran through the crowd, men looked at their neighbors, and eyes searched the balcony of the Fairweather House, which was black with spectators. The necktie party didn't know why, but it wanted John Slocum. It was nothing personal, just curiosity. But it isn't much more work to hang two men than one, and the advantage of a double hanging is that you don't have to think so much about the man you've just put out of the world when there are a pair of them. Justice is less personal in larger numbers.

Somebody had seen John Slocum riding out of town. Somebody said that he saw that Appaloosa of his up by the Swede's old claim, cutting across the sagebrush flats.

A warm glow passed through Jack Slade's chest at this piece of information. No man is totally alone, although a moment before he'd been feeling just that. He knew where Slocum was riding, and he knew why. He pursed his lips thoughtfully so that the smile he felt wouldn't show. He was cautious as a poker player with a cinch hand. He wanted everybody to behave normally. Bonnie would get him out of this. This damn bunch could never face the eyes of a good woman, no question about it. John Slocum had ridden to get her. Good old John. When he got out of this, he'd buy the man a drink and maybe even say thanks, although it wasn't a word that came easily to him.

"Well, then," Beidler said. "Let's get on with it."

It was Slade's turn to smile. He stretched his mouth as wide as it could go. "What's the hurry, Beidler? What's the big damn hurry?"

"Oh, no hurry, Jack. No hurry at all. The wheels of justice, you know, they grind slow, but they grind fine."

That image shook Jack Slade. He could almost see the grinding wheel. Like the wheat stone at the mill at the head of Lost Chance Gulch, it was tall as a man and wide as sixteen cartwheels, ten tons of hard-dressed stone on a stone platen, rolling very slowly. The grain could not withstand its deliberate progress. Although he'd been feeling sober for the last few minutes, the booze in his system came back at him all in a rush, and he weaved slightly and blinked. X. Beidler swam in his vision like a homunculus in a jar of green fluid. Only Beidler's smile was real.

"Come along, Jackie boy," Beidler crooned.

That snapped Slade back like a bullwhip. "Come where?" he demanded. Once again his hands fluttered at his sides. "I ain't no damn road agent."

"Well, that's for all of us to decide, isn't it, Jackie boy?"

"And stop calling me Jackie boy, Beidler. I ain't your son, and I ain't your punk, either."

One hand went up in placation. "Sure, Jack. Anything you say."

Slade asked, "How'd you like a third eye? Right between the other ones?" But he had no passion behind his words, and they fell lifeless as spit onto the board-walk.

Beidler came toward him, and Jack Slade couldn't remember how many bullets he had in his guns or what he meant to do with them.

Hell, two pistols wouldn't be much use against this crowd, anyway. There must have been three hundred men behind Beidler. Slade turned his head, and more men blocked his way down the street, although none of them stood as close as the little German, who had his hand out now and was saying, "Come along now, Jack. Let's have the revolvers. We wouldn't want anybody to get hurt, now, would we? If someone was to get hurt, someone else would have to hang for it, and that wouldn't do, would it? Somebody'd have to hang."

Slade didn't hand his pistols to X. Beidler, but he made no particular objection as Beidler's hands touched his flanks. Quickly, his flanks lost weight, and he felt giddy as a girl the first time she's been touched somewhere intimate, like something has been lost but something more has been gained.

Slade wondered why he'd never noticed the kindness in X. Beidler's eyes. He searched his memory for where he'd seen it before.

"Come along, Jack. We'll go down to the stable now and have our trial. Nothing disorderly, mind you. Everything done all legal and correct."

Slade tried a joke. "Why don't you just hang me here and have the trial afterward?" But his voice croaked, and his lips were dry. He feared that his hands were shaking, and so he tucked his thumbs behind his big belt buckle, the one that said "Wells Fargo Express" and had a picture of the strongbox he'd guarded so many times. The brass was reassuring under his thumbs.

Beidler answered his bad joke as if it had been meant seriously, saying that that sort of thing wasn't what the Vigilance Committee did. Slade wished very much that Beidler had laughed at his bad joke or groaned or said that it was a pitiful joke or had done anything except seriously explain the principles of the Vigilance Committee, as if Slade hadn't known what those principles were. It was like a damn mill wheel rolling toward him, indifferent to jokes, good or bad, indifferent to personalities, upright or lowdown. Jack Slade turned his head then, for the first time, and looked up the road toward the head of Alder Gulch, from where his wife and John Slocum would surely come.

* * *

Slocum's Appaloosa was a mountain horse. Bonnie
Slade's gelding was a flat racer, as fast as anything on the
great plains but more like a pounding machine than a trail
animal. Bonnie's horse roared along the sagebrush flats
full tilt, its head laboring up and down. Bonnie rode low
in the saddle, stretched out against the horse's neck, just
as she'd seen the Pony Express riders do. She melded
with her racing animal and gave him every help she
could. Her heels drummed against his side each time he
slowed and each time she feared that he might slow; it
was a steady tattoo, like her steady praying at the
animal's ear. "Come on, dearest. Come on, honey.
Come on, sweetheart."

Ahead, John Slocum's Appaloosa jumped left. Bonnie
hauled on her own reins, and her horse, less responsive,
leaned left. The sagebrush gave way, frighteningly and
quickly, to yellow rain-packed earth, bare as the moon.
A hole in the center of the patch of yellow earth that
Slocum's horse had skirted appeared, and hers had to
skirt it, too. She leaned far out to the side to help the
animal turn, and so she didn't see the hole flash by on the
horse's right, its hooves kicking pebbles into the old
shaft hole. Ten seconds after they passed, those pebbles
plunked into the water at the bottom of the shaft, where
there was no ear to hear them except for a pair of mine
rats.

The running beam that protruded from the front of the
stable was used to secure the block and tackle that hauled
hay off the wagons and through the narrow loft door just
below the single, thick block beam. The beam wasn't
quite square, being six inches on the horizontal and ten
inches on the vertical because most of the strain was
straight up and down; that's where the builders had put
most of the wood.

Beamis, Beidler's man, pulled the big sliding doors shut as if he were closing the backdrop for a theatrical performance. Slade was lifted up onto a feed bin that had been dragged out for that very purpose. The feed bin held eight bushels of shelled corn and was hammered together out of pine and lined with tin; it was a heavy affair, nearly four feet wide and six feet long. The accused stood with his feet at the level of most men's heads, and it seemed that he was already of a different kind than his accusers, an unintentional effect that had its uses.

Beidler stood on a lower box at Slade's right, and there was an empty crate on the left for witnesses.

The necktie party was warming up. More miners had abandoned their claims, and probably nobody worked at all in Virginia City except, of course, the Chinese, who were indifferent to the pranks of the white eyes.

Slade felt like he was on exhibit, like an animal mounted by a taxidermist, some creature caught and exhibited for its extraordinary qualities. He wanted to say that he wasn't that—that he was a man just like them, with his own fears and hopes and prayers—but he didn't want to say that. He was afraid that once he showed weakness, they'd kill him just so that they wouldn't be embarrassed by him anymore.

"I will set my eyes upon the hills, whence cometh my help" was what ran through Slade's head, and in another time it would have astonished him, because he wasn't a student of the Good Book. The crowd at his feet seemed awfully indistinct, almost as if he alone were alive and they were all dead, all ghosts. He had his hands folded neatly in front of his groin like a schoolboy making a scary recitation. He heard Beidler say something about accusers, but nobody stepped forward, and that was just as it should be. Slade felt light as goosedown in the wind. He felt almost like he could fly, like his mind might at any second find the magic combination of thoughts that would steal him away over the astonished faces of the crowd, leaving them staring up at the naked soles of his boots.

"Mr. Beidler, I will speak *for* the accused." It was Judge Batesworth's clear voice.

Slocum's horse veered hard left and then right at the prairie dog hill, twisting so suddenly that he nearly catapulted his rider. Slocum lost it for a moment. With his weight forward like a stupid piece of baggage, he was unable to help. It wasn't there before, he thought, although the prairie dog hill had been there before and he'd passed it right by, attentive only to the dangers of old mine shafts.

Slocum's horse missed most of the hill, which was half covered with sagebrush and wider than it first looked, nearly twenty feet in diameter. The Appaloosa raced across the edge of the circle, cutting an arc, while Slocum held his breath as he flew over twenty burrow entrances. Slocum didn't breathe as the tiny entrances flashed by under the horse's hooves, didn't breathe until his animal was on good ground again. Then he stood in the saddle, turning to wave Bonnie off, to turn her away from the peril that was already immersing her. Even as he watched, her horse charged dead across the widest center of the prairie dog town, flying, unable to turn or dodge. The front right shoulder dipped into something —some hole, some soft spot, some deep burrow whose inhabitants were pounded into a pulp by the iron hoof crashing through the ceiling of their safe den. The horse dipped that shoulder and strained to bring his foot out, to regain his stride. Bonnie was upright in the saddle, throwing her own weight to the rear, trying to brake the big animal before it tore itself to bits.

It didn't work.

Slowly, grandly, Bonnie's horse overran its own

imprisoned leg. With an odd, slow grace, it tucked its head down into its neck, and then the shoulder was crashing into the ground. Bonnie hadn't been rider enough to avoid the catastrophe, but she knew enough to kick her toes free of the stirrups. When the horse's neck crashed into the soft, tunneled earth, she was hurled over its head into the sagebrush. With the magnificence of a sinking ship, her horse's hindquarters rose above the flying woman and settled upon themselves.

Slocum shot her horse before he helped her onto the Appaloosa. It took only a half second, and he didn't think that a half second mattered now.

Judge Batesworth looked at the crowd of miners. He'd stood before these men a few times before, usually on the prosecutor's box that X. Beidler now occupied. Neither Beidler nor Slade watched the crowd. Slade was white-faced, scared silent, and Beidler had his penknife out and was digging casually at his fingernails.

The miners were hot for blood, not because they hated Slade, although he wasn't a popular fellow, but because an acquittal would mean that they'd wasted their time away from their claims, where they could be digging for nuggets that might make them rich. Men had found rich nuggets in this placer, some weighing twenty pounds. A few men were already casting anxious glances back up the hill, where claim jumpers could be settling in right now.

Batesworth knew that he had to be swift. "I don't like this man, Jack Slade, any better than you do," he began.

Jack Slade looked down at the judge with murderous eyes, as if the man who was trying to save him had to love him, too.

"But he's no road agent. Not one man here has been robbed by him. No road agent has accused him, and you all know how they like to chatter when the mood's upon them."

That brought a laugh. The only time the road agents became talkative was when the rope around their neck threatened to close off their speech forever. Every man in the crowd was familiar with that phenomenon.

"How about Little Jimmy?" somebody hollered. Maybe it was some friend of Little Jimmy, maybe somebody who hadn't seen a hanging in a while.

"Jimmy Eads was an outlaw, and Jack Slade killed him. Nobody can deny that."

"Took his damn time about it, too." It was a different voice this time.

Judge Batesworth put one hand in the air to quell the groundswell of sympathy. "Little Jimmy Eads got what was coming to him, and there isn't a man here who can say he didn't deserve it."

That quelled the talk, but Slade just had to get his two cents in. "Jimmy Eads was a road agent," he said, as seriously as a child explaining that Jimmy was a bad man.

"Well, you ain't Jesus Christ come to save us," some wit got in quickly, and somebody else hooted.

The judge reached over to touch Slade and warn him against speaking in his own defense, but he couldn't touch anything but Slade's legs, and they weren't that intimate. "Men of the Committee of Vigilance. Until this day, your work has been honorable, and I've been proud to be part of the grim but necessary work. If the territory is ever to become a civilized state in the Union, we must clean out these murderers and thieves. So long as there is no law, we have to make our own law, and until this day, it's been good law, too. Think of the men we've done for. Men like Gallagher and George Ives, Plummer and Dave Bell. We've pursued the guilty, and we've hung them, too, and by God, it's our proudest boast that we never made a mistake. Remember Dave Bell's last words in Nevada City when he asked for the list of men we'd hanged. We gave it to him name by name, and he declared, 'Boys, there's not an honest man on the list.' And he spoke knowing he was about to meet his maker, the judge of men's souls.''

Some of the miners at the back of the crowd were getting restless. There was work to be done and nobody doing it. One man hauled his watch out of his pocket and consulted it.

Slocum's Appaloosa was game, but no horse can carry double long. John Slocum weighed 200 pounds naked, and his equipment made 30 pounds more. Bonnie Slade's 105 pounds was almost more extra weight than the strong-hearted horse could carry. She tried. She raced on across the sagebrush flat as fast as she could, but her stride wasn't so soft and easy, and her gallop, usually her smoothest gait, was pretty rocky. The sweat flew back off her neck and splashed against Slocum's arms, and he felt the horse's laboring through the reins. "Good girl! Good girl! Just run now, damn you!" Encouraged, the horse stretched out her ears and picked up the pace for another hundred yards or so.

Bonnie Slade rode Slocum's blanket roll, which was a pretty damned uncomfortable seat, with her legs pressed tight and the horse's legs flying up like they meant to hit her. She was able to hang on only by wrapping her arms around Slocum's middle and pressing her face against his back. His shirt was soaked with sweat, and it smelled like horse sweat, like her own sweat; it was all great effort, all work. The Appaloosa had lost some of her agility and wasn't veering so wide or so fast around the prospect holes and hidden mine shafts. She careered down into one and luckily out the other side; the prospector had given up after digging just inches into the earth.

Burdened with double the weight she usually carried, the horse jumped a mine shaft. Although she landed three-legged with one leg down in the hole, the forward momentum carried her on. Her leg came up, and she hardly broke stride. Slocum saw the danger. The horse knew the danger. To Bonnie Slade, it was a break in stride and a blur.

Jack Slade was developing a very great admiration for Judge Batesworth. Once they turned him loose, he'd buy the judge a drink. He wouldn't buy a whole bottle, because the judge would be uncomfortable drinking a whole bottle with the notorious Jack Slade. Hell, the judge had a teenage son; maybe the boy would like pistol lessons. From everything that happens to you, you can learn something, Jack Slade was thinking. He thought that he'd try bringing Bonnie into town more often, because, come to think of it, he'd been selfish, spending all his money on booze. A man had to have a drink, no question about that, but he'd overdone it. He'd hold back more from now on, maybe spend a little more time at the house with Bonnie. Hell, maybe she could teach him to read. Funny, it had never occurred to him before. The crowd was thinning at the edges as Judge Batesworth recited the list of the committee's achievements and insisted that this hanging would diminish that proud record, not enhance it. The judge had a way with words. So far he hadn't said "damn" once, which was some kind of record in this country.

"I ask you to set this man free," he said. "When I began to speak, I thought we could offer him simple banishment, because, as you all know, Jack Slade hasn't been the best neighbor in the world."

There was a laugh.

Jack Slade felt the need to add, "That's right, I ain't." He meant to be funny, but it came out as a boast. The crowd stopped leaving. Men looked at one another.

Jack shrugged and avoided the judge's angry eyes. Like most bad men, Jack was just a very bad boy with the strength and armor of a man.

There was a rustle in the crowd at his feet. Jack Slade thought that it was funny how different men looked when you saw them from a new angle, like the man climbing on Beidler's box. You'd never know that old MacArdle was so bald on top or that his skull was so covered with freckles. Down from his perch, Beidler grinned up at Jack Slade like the cat who'd eaten the canary.

Slade said, "Fuck you," but he kept it low, under his breath.

MacArdle began by clearing his throat.

"Got a cold, Mac?" Slade asked.

MacArdle wouldn't look at him. "He's ruined me," he said. He stood like a stick and spoke loudly but without much inflection. "I try and run the best place here in Virginia City. Man has to go out and have some fun now and again, and I've always sought to run a decent place for you to do it. I serve honest measure and the best quality I can get freighted in."

Only Slade heard Beidler's whisper. "Get to the point, man. Don't promote your saloon."

"He's ruined me. He's ruined my life. He comes in any damn time he feels like it, and he shoots the place up. Nobody wants to drink at my place because Slade's likely to show up and put a bullet into him. Hell, boys, think of how you'd feel if Shotgun Slade came around your claim and started wrecking things."

"I always paid!" Slade was outraged.

MacArdle rose to the occasion. "How many men would like their things shot up just because the gunman would pay them back later? Men, he's ruined my life!"

He stopped and flushed. He had moisture in the corners of his eyes. He realized that all he'd said was true.

Those tears had precisely opposite effects: Slade smiled to see them. Through the long afternoon when Little Jimmy had died, Jimmy hadn't wept once, and that fact was the only thing Slade had ever credited to Jimmy's account. He died like a man, without whining or crying. When Slade saw the tears staining MacArdle's chalky cheeks, he grinned. MacArdle wasn't a man any longer, and nobody would listen to him now.

Some of the miners who'd been leaving came back. Others who'd been getting restless stayed still.

"Men, my saloon is my home. I spend all my waking hours inside that saloon so it'll be a decent place for gents to come and relax. I roust the whores out, and I don't allow ruffians. When the doors open at eight in the morning for those who need a pick-me-up—and there's many of us who've needed a stiff shot to face a hard decision or a bad day—it's me that opens them, and like as not, I have to follow after the swamper so the floor's clean and the glassware sparkles. At eleven o'clock I set out the free lunch, and all my hams are sugar-cured, and all my fried chicken is cooked up special in the back of Wing Fong's restaurant, and the beef is from the round, and I supervise the corning myself. It's a good lunch, men, and it's free to anyone who orders a single glass of nickel beer. Ain't it a good lunch? Ain't it?"

X. Beidler took the rope from the man who'd been carrying it and ran his fingers along the thirteen knots, tugging at each one.

"What the hell does a free lunch have to do with a man's life?" Judge Batesworth shouted.

His shout sent a chill down Slade's spine. His curse sounded impossibly raw in Slade's ears, impossibly harsh, like the cawing of a crow. Frantically he searched through his memory but couldn't remember the last time the judge had used improper language.

MacArdle stood on the low box, with tears streaming down his face and a stunned expression in his eyes. He raised his hand in a fist. He cried out, "The pickles. I get the best sour pickles myself, and I put them out on the bar from eleven-thirty in the morning until two-thirty. Who else has a free lunch like that? Who?"

Slade shifted his feet. "Oh, Jesus Christ," he said softly. Was this any damn reason for a man to die?

John Slocum had had horses shot out from under him. He'd laid horses down to serve as makeshift forts to fight off a band of Indians, and he'd lost horses to that old cavalry trick. He never thought too much of the horse's intelligence, which he rated as low, or its interest in humankind, because he thought that interest was minimal. Yet countless times in the roughest crossings, his horse had eaten better than he did. Slocum's horse was still eating oats when his own belly was growling against his backbone. Soaked from a wet winter storm or half frozen, as soon as Slocum got into shelter, he'd care for the horse first. Even when he was faint with cold and sickness, he rubbed down his animal. He'd used his shirt for the job when there wasn't anything else available.

It was as close to a code of ethics as he had. He owned the best horses and gave them the best care. Despite his estimate of their intelligence and affective possibilities, he talked to them like they were dear friends who understood every word he said, because there was no use thinking worse of the animal than you had to.

He slammed his hard-heeled stockman's boots into the Appaloosa's flanks and listened to the animal's labored breathing. He'd traded for this horse with a band of roving Nez Perce, giving them a good Sharps rifle and two pounds of plug tobacco, which was all he had had.

The horse was eighteen hands high, big barreled, heavy through the forequarters, with hindquarters as finely formed as those of an Arabian. The mare's head was huge and, except for its fine gray color and limpid black eyes, hopelessly ugly. He'd owned this horse six months now and had never tried it so hard before, a dead run across bad ground, carrying double. Still the horse kept its stride.

Slocum felt the woman's face pressed against his back, and it didn't seem like her face was very large, as he sawed the reins wildly to keep the horse from hurtling into disaster. Narrowly, the Appaloosa dodged another prospect hole, which up close wasn't as deep as it had seemed and would have been less exhausting to cross than to avoid. The horse stretched out on the other side, racing toward the top of Alder Gulch, and John Slocum wondered why he was ruining the best horse he'd owned in five years for a man like Jack Slade. Sometimes it happens that way.

Judge Batesworth was crying that they shouldn't sully the fine record of the committee, but the crowd was pressing down the hill toward the stable to get a good view. Slade was grinning like a fool. MacArdle was still weeping like his heart would break.

"Don't run out of tears, MacArdle," Slade said. "I like to see a grown man cry about a lunch. Hell, when I get out of this fix, I'll give you a free lunch." He dropped his voice, but MacArdle wasn't having any of that. He pointed his finger and cried shrilly, "Did you hear that? Did you hear? He says he's going to kill me. Which of you would like to be in my place?"

Beidler climbed onto the platform beside Jack Slade. No trace of a smile flickered across his lips. He spoke so that only Slade could hear. "Jack, I'm afraid it's all over with you. Now, you don't want to disgrace yourself. Go out of this life the same way you lived it, as a man. I never once heard anybody say you wasn't a man."

Slade felt pretty good. He felt like punching the little German off the box. That'd be pretty funny. With difficulty he restrained himself. "Jump or slide, eh, Beidler?"

Beidler smiled back at him, a smile of perfect understanding. "Correct, my friend. Bend your neck."

That simple gesture may seem like the easiest thing in the world, but it isn't. Slade's vertebrae seemed locked together, unable to move, and he had to force himself to bow his head. When he raised his head again, with the rope around his neck, Jack Slade was a genuinely changed man.

Plenty of hangings go that way, although not many people ever get close enough to see it. X. Beidler had been the only confidant and sole companion of a good many hanged men, and he never doubted for a moment the reality of these conversions. They were genuine, he was sure of that. Now, how long they'd last, that was a different matter. And of course, the conversion might save a man's soul, but it didn't undo the evil he'd done or disinter the corpses he'd created.

X. Beidler wasn't nearly as surprised by Jack Slade's change as Jack himself was. Why didn't I see how it would end? Slade thought. These men wished to hang him because they didn't understand that the Jack Slade they were going to kill was not the same man who'd terrified MacArdle and a dozen other men. If he had to do it over again, he would even have turned Little Jimmy Eads over to the Vigilance Committee and foresworn his own revenge.

The miners were pressing down the hill and pushing so hard that the men in front turned and pushed back. For a second it looked like a melee was about to start.

"You gents don't have any respect, yes?" X. Beidler

asked, and his Germanic accent came through like it usually didn't. The "yes" was a hiss and about as amiable as a snake's; it stopped the fight before it had a chance to get going.

Jack Slade was trying desperately to think of words to say, but his tongue was thick and his mouth bone dry. Beamis had slipped up into the loft of the stable and was inching out on the beam. Somebody else tossed the coiled rope up, and for an instant it looked like the rope had gone wide, far beyond Beamis's straining fingers. But he caught the coil, and the crowd cheered.

Beamis didn't run the rope through the block and tackle, as Beidler had intended, but just draped it across the beam and let it fall to willing hands below. On the beam, the rope ran right against the heavy bolts that secured the block.

"You got any last words?" Beidler asked Slade.

Slade's eyes bugged out, and he opened his mouth. He had a mental picture of Bonnie. He was no murderer. She'd tell them that they had no reason to string him up. "My wife," he croaked.

Beidler cocked his head curiously and then said, "Yes, we'll bring you to her afterward."

"For God's sake, man," Slade yelled. "Let me say good-bye to my wife." His shout echoed, and it went to the hearts of many of the miners. If Beidler hadn't given the command to haul away, they probably would have waited, and Bonnie Slade might have saved her husband's life.

The rope tautened as six men pulled on it. They hauled Jack Slade up to his tiptoes, and there it stuck, jammed against the bolt far above them. Slade had his fingers under the rope, and he was on his very tiptoes, but he wasn't going up any farther. His face turned red and then black, and the men hauled as hard as they could, but the rope was totally jammed. Jack's toes danced on the wooden box like the toes of a ballerina, and his hands clutched at the rope. He stayed that way for a minute, two minutes, until Beidler called, "Let him down, damn it."

The men on the end of the rope let it down, and Beamis hurried out on the beam and freed the rope.

Jack Slade had a very strange look in his eyes, and he said, "By God, boys, you're strangling me."

"Heave!"

Although they might have spared him before the first attempt, they wouldn't spare him once they'd started, because Jack Slade was beyond the last point where men can turn back.

Fearing that he'd stick again, six men really put their backs into it this time, and Jack Slade sailed up above their heads like a flag. He was limp. His neck broke, and the questions were already going out of his eyes.

Slocum's Appaloosa was snorting pink sputum as she raced down the road past the abandoned claims on upper Alder Gulch. They came into view of the stable just as Jack sailed up into the air like a soul released from earthly bondage. Slocum winced.

This was no good reason to ruin a good horse.

Bonnie Slade screamed eerily, the cry of a child. "Jack. Oh, my God. Jack!"

Her cry penetrated the crowd. The miners turned and scrambled to get out of the way of the horse with the blood pouring from its nostrils and the woman screaming like a banshee on its back.

Gathered at the foot of the makeshift scaffold were the judge, several lawyers, a couple of horse doctors, the painless dentist, the man who owned the hardware store, half a dozen prosperous saloonkeepers including MacArdle, and, of course, X. Beidler.

Bonnie's frantic eyes raced from face to face, looking for a message.

They were the men of stature of the community. They were the men who read books and held political discussions. They were the civilized men. She screamed. The world had turned upside down, and Jack was swinging high above her. She swore that she heard some sounds from him.

"Oh, God," she cried. "Please cut him down. Save him. He's trying to talk."

But Jack was beyond that. The sounds she took for speech were the grumblings of his belly and his gut relaxing. Men were moving from underneath, because it was about to get smelly and wet.

"He's still alive. Save him." The figure danced far above her, and she slid off the horse as Slocum drew rein. She hit the ground pretty hard, but she was limp and didn't feel a thing.

5

MacArdle and his two relief bartenders were doing a land-office business. It isn't hard to move whiskey. MacArdle's excellent free lunch was very much in evidence on the bar, and miners jostled one another to get a slice of ham or beef, as if by eating here today they were consummating some rite the origins of which they didn't quite understand. The food was the same as always, and men ate or did not eat, not so much according to their appetites but according to how they felt about Jack Slade. His friends weren't hungry; his enemies had beef in their mouths and potato salad in their gullets, and they washed the whole mess down with heavy glasses of Centennial beer.

The miners were crammed into MacArdle's saloon from the bar to the back wall. They were testy, as men seemed to get after a necktie party, but they were unwilling to seek discharge for their testiness in an old-fashioned brawl. This afternoon a man could insult his worst enemy with impunity. Shootings always lead to other shootings, but hangings make hard men as gentle as lambs.

MacArdle had all the business in town. The other saloons only got his overflow. He was sweating and happy and praised Jack Slade every chance he had, as if

Slade had conferred great favors on him. MacArdle was more than happy to call Slade a friend.

"Another bottle down here, Jacob!"

"Isn't it about time for a house round?"

"Sure. Sure thing." Custom in the bars dictated that every third round was on the house. It was an ingenious custom, because nobody liked to leave after his second drink with a free one on the way, and nobody felt quite right leaving right after a free drink. A drinker could leave gracefully after drink number five, but then he'd again be walking out on a free one.

"On the house, gents. Drink up."

Most of the prosperous men who had gathered in MacArdle's saloon were upset by the afternoon's hanging, but that is the natural response to the sight of a pair of feet you've helped to put high in the air, and those who'd attended necktie parties before were used to it.

One bunch, at the table right in front of Lillie Langtry, had caught a pilgrim: a dude, a tenderfoot so new to the country that he didn't carry a sidearm. He sat at the back table and told everyone within earshot how he'd never seen anything like the goings-on here this afternoon, and he didn't mind who knew it. The men who sat at his table and drank his whiskey were basking in the glow of his admiration. The more they basked, the harder they got, until, to listen to them, you would have thought that the reason Jack Slade wasn't hanged earlier or didn't get hanged twice a day was that they were too busy elsewhere stringing up bad hats.

They spoke of other hangings. Several told the tenderfoot the jump or slide joke, and he was suitably impressed because he could identify with Dave Gallagher, another reader, another Easterner much like himself, and he could imagine himself in that slippery hayloft, trying to go out like a man, though he hadn't lived as one for very many years.

The tenderfoot bought another bottle in memory of Dave Gallagher, which offended one or two of the men who'd helped string Dave up; they went to another table, and the quality of guests at the tenderfoot's table declined, with the professionals getting replaced by roustabouts and other low types who'll always find a fool with a free bottle. When the tenderfoot offered to buy a bottle for Jack Slade, his remark was thought to be so tasteless that even these types gave him a wide berth. Soon all the other chairs at his table were empty or spirited away to fill out other tables where regulars drank.

The regulars were of two minds. One mind said that killing Jack Slade was the beginning of order, that Slade's public execution made civilization more welcome in Virginia City. That mind pictured the swinging body against a backdrop of churches, schools for youngsters, and women walking tree-lined streets safe and unmolested. That mind dreamed of an East that never was, except as a dream, and a West that could never be. The other mind thought about Jack Slade's few moments of fame on the scaffold and imagined itself on that same scaffold with the rope around its neck. What would I say, what could I do? The first mind drank hard, because the more booze it put away, the clearer seemed the outlines of that civilized Virginia City, a place for honest men and women. The second mind drank to forget what it had seen and what it could imagine.

Normally, the party started to dwindle at nine o'clock in MacArdle's, except on Saturday nights or the Fourth of July or when they had horse racing up and down Main Street. First the merchants would go home, then the judges and the lawyers and sawbones and dentists. The miners went last of all, which was odd, since they worked harder than the other classes of men and rose the earliest. Tonight, everyone was interested in closing MacArdle's with the owner. It was odd. The drink flowed, and around eleven o'clock MacArdle had to send one of his bartenders up the street to the Bullwhacker, where the Yellow Kid presided over an empty establishment. When the fresh barrel of beer came rolling down the street, the Yellow Kid came with it.

MacArdle's glowed with light, like a beacon calling them on. They rolled the borrowed barrel in the street because the boardwalk was too narrow. After the barrel had picked up a sheen of horse droppings, the fastidious Yellow Kid refused to touch it anymore, and so they slowed down and stopped before Mother Sue's whorehouse to borrow a few pairs of gloves. Mother Sue had a handyman whose fingers were about the right size, and she was curious about the goings-on at MacArdle's and burning with some news of her own about the recently widowed Mrs. Slade.

The Yellow Kid urged the madam to bring herself, her girls, and her information where it would all be appreciated. The Yellow Kid appreciated Mother Sue's bosom and bustle and hoped to have some of each before the night was out. Mother Sue, though nominally a competitor of the Kid's—he collected for the cribs behind the Bullwhacker—considered herself and her girls as ladies of a slightly higher plane, and besides, she liked the Kid's style.

"The hell with MacArdle," she announced. "Let's bring him his beer."

Mother Sue trailed down the boardwalk with her flock of doves giggling behind and MacArdle's bartender rolling fifty gallons of beer and cursing the Yellow Kid, who, with one hand in Mother Sue's and the other on her bustle, said that he had much better things to do.

MacArdle wasn't happy to see them. Mother Sue was far too brassy for his establishment, and besides, he had his memories of the other night and his pride. His pride vanished when he noticed the youngest member of Mother Sue's flock, half hidden by a couple of her coarser sisters. MacArdle walked over and served the women himself. He was brusque, to show them their place; and unctuous, to show them his.

They all drank beer because they were ladies, after all, and here socially, not to pick up tricks. The miners who'd screwed them on Saturday nights were surprised at their lack of ardor on a night when they intended to sleep alone. MacArdle kept casting sly glances at the girl of his choice, and once or twice she returned them. In a special bin under the bar, MacArdle had two bottles of champagne. The bottles were warm, but they were genuine Monopole. He'd brought them in two years before for a wedding that hadn't come off. He wondered whether Mother Sue's youngest—her name was Bess —would enjoy a little champagne and a little reading of the Good Book in his quarters upstairs. He'd won everything else he wanted today, so why not her? Absently, his hand caressed his balls. Bess the child-whore understood, and she smiled at him, a smile so knowing and lewd that he blushed and turned away.

"Round on the house," he called gaily.

There was the usual crunch at the bar as men found their free whiskey.

Mother Sue was talking. "Cut him down herself. She wouldn't let nobody help her. Not that one." There was a certain exasperation in Mother Sue's voice because "that one" was too proud and not entirely sensible. "Oh, she had somebody to catch Jack's body once she cut the rope, a man by the name of Slocum, green-eyed fellow who looks to be quick with a Colt. He handled old Jack easy as a baby, though Jack must have weighed plenty, and you know how heavy dead meat is."

MacArdle moved down the bar again. He wanted to

keep an eye on the young whore. He wouldn't offer her any money. He didn't hold with whores. He'd read to her from the Book, from the Song of Solomon: "Her two breasts are like two deer who feed among the lilies." He wouldn't use her as a whore. He wondered what tricks she knew how to do. He thought that she'd know some interesting ones. She caught his eye and winked, a wink of such bawdiness that he answered it in kind.

Mother Sue had a circle of eager listeners, mostly men who'd held back at the edges of the crowd. Men who'd actually hauled poor Jack off the ground weren't so interested in learning what had happened to his remains. "So she had Jack strapped across the back of an Appaloosa mare, and it must have been the one she rode in on, because it was a tuckered horse if I ever saw one. Wouldn't be surprised if the animal didn't live the night. The two of them went up the street past Dugan's to Red Marco's place. Red's where I got my information." Mother Sue flounced. "Direct from the horse's mouth. You know what she wanted done?"

Her listeners shook their heads.

"She wanted Jack Slade pickled, that's what she wanted. All the blood drained out of him and popped down into a barrel of trade whiskey."

Someone called out, "Hell, old Jack'd love that."

There was laughter. Someone else added that now Jack Slade was inside of the same whiskey that he'd long been putting himself outside of. That was too complex for a good laugh so late at night, but it rated a chuckle.

"Said she was sending him back to St. Louis," Mother Sue continued. "Bring me a drink of whiskey, and make it rye whiskey, MacArdle. I hate that damn old trade whiskey, myself."

"Jack ever come by your place?"

"Him? No. He wasn't like most married men. I guess

he figured he had plenty enough at home to keep him busy."

Men produced grins of complicity. One man pinched one of Mother Sue's girls and was quite unprepared for the glare he got for his trouble.

"My doves ain't workin' tonight," Mother Sue said to avoid further misunderstanding. "We're in here to drink and to mourn Jack Slade, who knew how to keep it in his pants except when his wife wanted it." She paused, screwed up her face for comic effect, and drawled in a deep whiskey tenor, "Wonder what she knows that I don't?"

If MacArdle hadn't been feeling so splendid, so much like he and that young whore would spend the night together, he would have objected to the note of vulgarity, which normally wasn't welcome in his saloon.

"Here's to Jack Slade, inside his barrel of whiskey, curled up just like a baby in the womb. Here's to one man who never used a woman hard."

"Or a man easy," MacArdle muttered. He couldn't help himself and was caught by the laughter that greeted his sally, acknowledging it with a slow smile.

The young whore showed her teeth at his unintentional wit, and he thought how wonderful those teeth would feel nibbling on him.

Bonnie Slade sat on the second-story balcony of the Fairweather Inn. The management had put a row of rockers on the blacony for guests, and usually men sat and rocked and chatted until the moon came up. Tonight everybody was at MacArdle's. Slocum rolled himself a quirly and fired it up. The flame illuminated his calm face and strong hands.

Bonnie Slade said, "I'm sorry about your horse."

"Yes," he said, taking it no larger or smaller than was necessary. It had been a good horse, and he'd liked it, but it was at the renderer's now, and there wasn't much sense dwelling on it. It was going to be one of those brilliant nights. The Navajos have a legend that the Milky Way is the stars spilled by Coyote across the heavens; and in the fall it's easy to imagine Coyote, the sloppy painter, doing just that.

John Slocum had his boots on the rail. Once they'd hauled Jack up to Red Marco's fine establishment and gotten him offloaded, he'd taken his horse down to the little man at the foot of the gulch. The knacker's yard was piles of old meat and animal remnants and great vats of boiling hooves and bones. The man gave him $10 for a horse that had been worth $200 that morning, and Slocum patted her cheek and put a bullet behind her ear. Slocum told himself that she was just a horse, after all, but she had given him her last full measure of service, and he hadn't liked his way of showing gratitude. He didn't think that Jack Slade's friendship was worth a good horse dead, but that was all past. He had his boots up and could hear the sounds of laughter from MacArdle's saloon up the street, the clink of glasses, a woman's shriek of amusement.

"Well," he said.

She didn't help him out. She just sat in her rocking chair, feet slightly spread, not rocking, looking out at the street or in at herself—it wasn't easy to tell.

Slocum drew in a deep lungful of smoke and coughed. "What are you going to do next?" he asked.

"Same as I have been doing," she replied with more asperity than he thought he deserved. A moment later, she added, "I will continue learning. I will continue my education."

"Uh-huh." He stopped for a minute. "What're you thinkin' on doin' for a living?" He had a pound of gold in his poke from the poker game that morning and figured that he'd give her some of it to see her to Utah or back east or wherever she wanted to go. There were three jobs in Virginia City for a woman: seamstress, wife, and whore. Only the seamstress had her choice of when she took her clothes off.

"I have some resources," she said. "Jack had almost $50 in his pockets when . . . when. . . ."

"Fifty dollars won't go too far."

"I have his weapons, and I suppose they'll fetch a good price. Jack always took care of his weapons, and I suppose they'll have a certain added value as curiosities."

"I suppose so."

Slocum knew that when Bill Thompson was gunned down in Tombstone, his twin ivory-handled Colts brought $100 each. Bill's guns were fine guns and worth at least $30 each, but they surely weren't worth $200. Slocum never understood the interest some people took in a dead man's guns, as if owning the guns made you a little part of the dead man, and whoever got Slade's Remington Double Action revolvers would have a little piece of Jack Slade. It never worked that way with a dead man's boots or braces or underwear. Slocum wondered why the widow couldn't sell Jack Slade's underwear as easily as his guns, but let go of that thought because it was pretty bitter. It wasn't his spouse lying in a whiskey barrel up at Marco's. Hell, Jack hadn't even been much of a friend, and as a human being he couldn't hold a candle to the woman he'd wedded.

John Slocum's bitterness was there because he knew for certain that one day he'd be lying in some street somewhere with his mouth stopped up with dust while the jackals and vultures bartered for his guns.

"I want to thank you for helping me," she said with no intonation whatever. "I'm sorry you had to destroy your horse."

"Not so sorry as she was," Slocum drawled. He could

do with a drink, but he didn't want to do his drinking at MacArdle's tonight, because everybody would be asking about the failed rescue, and he didn't think that he could put up with that. He shifted slightly in his rocker. He grunted.

"Why was Jack the way he was?" Bonnie Slade asked.

"Jesus Christ," Slocum said. "Jesus Christ."

She was implacable. "Why did he drink so much and hurt so many people? He had a loving streak in him. I've seen it. Times when he'd carry the water up from the creek or wash the dishes. Once he brought me a bonnet back from town, and it was as new as could be. It was a pink bonnet, and I've always preferred blue, but it was a kind thought."

"Don't know what makes us how we are. All dealt different cards. Jack was dealt fewer hands than most."

She turned to face him, and her face had a kind of questioning light in it. "Is that all, Mr. Slocum?"

"John."

"Is that all there is to it? Do we play a game well or badly and then at some point find outselves dealt out?"

He shrugged. He didn't often think about matters like this and wouldn't have sought the discussion if it had been up to him.

"Please, John. Answer me."

"I don't know, Bonnie. I don't know what made a man like Jack any more than I know what makes a woman like you."

"A woman like me?"

"Well, you ain't exactly common, you know. Readin' books all the time. Runnin' off with Jack Slade."

She tried out a small smile. "But he was the only man who'd take me."

"I reckon many a man would've taken you," Slocum said.

"Not from my husband. How do you roll those cigarettes?"

He was surprised but made his instruction as careful as possible. "You just crimp the paper here along the fold and sprinkle in a line of tobacco and then moisten her like this and roll her up."

She held the roll-your-own between her fingers, studying it. She asked him for a light, and he scratched a lucifer along his boot to oblige her.

She dragged on the quirly and coughed. Gamely, she puffed again. "It makes me dizzy," she said. "Does it make you dizzy?"

"Not once you get used to it."

"What are they doing in MacArdle's saloon?"

Now it was his turn to cough, his turn to shrug. She seemed to have plenty of questions that he couldn't or didn't want to answer. "They're just drinkin' and braggin'. Same as always."

"Do they hang a man every afternoon?"

"No, I reckon they don't."

"There must be thirty horses at the hitch rail. See, there are so many men inside that some must stand outside the doors. What did you think of my husband, John?"

Jesus. "I, uh, I thought he was funny sometimes. I thought he'd never backshoot a friend."

"Well. That isn't much to put on an epitaph," she said.

"Look. What do you want to hear?"

"I want to hear the truth."

"Jack was a rough man. He hoorawed the wrong man once too often, and they strung him up. Nobody besides you is likely to mourn him."

Her voice, when she finally spoke, was thinner than it had been. "Well, I asked for that, didn't I?"

"And you'll be better off without him," Slocum added.

There was a long pause. She puffed on her quirly. He saw its glow. It glowed when she threw it down on the street below.

"Yes. I suppose I will be. But that doesn't cancel my debts to him."

"What debts? Marriage always seemed like an even trade to me."

"For someone who doesn't like to answer questions, you seem to have some strong opinions, Mr. Slocum." She spoke very sweetly.

He set his feet flat. He looked at her face, which was quite lovely and very strange in the moonlight. He said, "I don't reckon you want to hear anything I have to say, which is okay, but don't worry me with questions, then."

Her eyes searched his face. Finally she said, "Perhaps I haven't thanked you enough for what you tried to do today."

"What in the hell is that supposed to mean?" Slocum asked.

"You know, John. I don't know. I hardly know what it means. Perhaps I should give you my body."

He grinned at her. "Supposin' I'd take it."

Now that was a surprise. "But . . . I thought. . . . Both my husbands, they wanted me."

Slocum answered dryly. "I ain't them."

"No, I suppose not. Mr. Slocum, would you do me a service?"

"Likely would."

"Accompany me across the street. I feel a need for spirits."

"I could bring a bottle back up here. That way, nobody'd be botherin' you."

She gave him a smile. "Perhaps, after today, I need to be bothered. Perhaps I crave the diversion."

"Suit yourself."

Slocum never thought that he could live anybody's life for him, but this was one of the times he'd have liked to try. In his room, he lit the kerosene lamp and saw to his shirt and inspected his two Colt Navys. The caps were all

THE NECKTIE PARTY 103

right, and the charges were dry. A silent Bonnie Slade watched him as he inspected the weapons, but she kept mum. She carried one of the enormous reticules that had been the style five years ago back east.

As they crossed Main Street, he was wondering what next, where next. He had a grubstake now, a good one. Maybe he'd go up north toward the border the Indians called the Medicine Line. It was rough country up there, he'd heard, and not too many whites had seen it since the French traders and mountain men. Maybe he'd ride north for a spell and see some new country. Virginia City left a slightly sour taste in his mouth.

A dozen men stood outside MacArdle's, mostly drunk, with several bottles in evidence. One man started toward Bonnie Slade because she was young and pretty, and he was drunk.

"Careful, partner," Slocum said. It was a warning rattle, pure, simple, and automatic. The man stepped hurriedly back.

"Sorry, ma'am. I didn't recognize. . . ."

The apology was genuine. Bonnie Slade was a virtuous woman and known as such, and no man trifled with her without inviting the community's wrath. A man could do pretty much anything he liked with Mother Sue's girls, at least until he ran into another man who was bigger and stronger and had his own ideas about what to do. But with a woman known to be virtuous, bothering her was a hanging offense. The drunk repeated his apology, his eyes watering as he attempted coherence.

It was eleven o'clock, and MacArdle's crowd had changed. The classier citizens had gone home. The hard-drinking miners were still going strong, and Mother Sue's doves were having a pretty good time, too, flirting and dancing now and again when a miner could be persuaded to pick up the squeeze-box. The girls felt luxurious because they were in MacArdle's classy saloon tonight and wouldn't be allowed back tomorrow. They were enjoying it in the meantime.

Mother Sue was sloppy drunk, seated at the table in front of Lillie Langtry, whom she'd seen once on a tour. The Yellow Kid had his hand inside her blouse and was openly fondling her breasts. The tenderfoot was shocked by the open lasciviousness but fascinated, too, and didn't want to move.

At the bar, MacArdle's young whore was getting plenty of attention from the saloonkeeper, who had decided that this might well be his day and night. She seemed friendly enough, quite friendly. MacArdle thought that she was attracted to him precisely because of his shyness. He wanted to believe that his Bible reading had had a good effect on her soul. He liked her sharp teeth.

The woman who sat beside her was more plainly dressed than the young whore but was a looker, too. "What'll you have?"

The woman turned to her male escort. "Two whiskeys. Rye whiskey and a couple glasses of water to chase the whiskey down."

"I'll have a water chaser, too, MacArdle," the young whore said, taking Bonnie Slade's choice as a reproach.

With a grumble that women were getting a sight too fancy for the saloon, MacArdle brought the drinks and made a second trip for the water.

MacArdle didn't recognize Bonnie Slade, because he hadn't expected her. He had seen her from time to time in town. When he put the glass of water before her, she tossed off the drink like it was honey water instead of the rough stuff it was. She lifted the glass of water and wordlessly hurled it in his face.

She said calmly, "I'll have another glass of water, if you please, Mr. MacArdle. I seem to have spilled mine."

MacArdle stopped, frozen. "Mrs. Slade. . . ."

"Mr. MacArdle, Mr. Slocum. I presume you've met."

Slocum smiled at MacArdle in a wolfish way, but MacArdle was too confused to heed the introduction. Stupidly, he repeated, "Mrs. Slade."

"Yes. I am Jack Slade's widow, and I was formerly his wife. I understand that it was your complaint that got my Jack hanged."

"Who told you that?"

"Common knowledge, Mr. MacArdle." That was true enough. The mortician Marco had told her because he was a garrulous man and wanted to say something more than the usual condolences.

"Jack Slade was no friend of mine." MacArdle set his chin stubbornly.

The young whore licked her lips and clapped her hands. "Bravo, MacArdle. Bravo."

Heartened, he said, "Mrs. Slade, I'm sorry for your loss, but Virginia City is a safer place to live and work."

"Safer for who, Mr. MacArdle?" She cocked her head, expectant as a sparrow.

"Why, safer for the ordinary citizens, Mrs. Slade. Safer for those of us who hope, by our manner and example, to make something of Virginia City, to make it into—"

"The Athens of the West?" She smiled. "Last winter I read Plato's *Apology*. You know the work. They condemn Socrates to death, though he's more just than his accusers."

Stiffly he replied, "I'm afraid I'm not familiar with that, madam."

"Ah, then perhaps you meant to turn Virginia City into the Camelot of the West. You remember King Arthur's court city, of course."

"I'm afraid I'm not familiar with the gentleman, ma'am."

"I see. You do not read."

"No, ma'am. I don't count reading among my recreations."

"No? Yet you seem to have a very good idea what civilization is, Mr. MacArdle."

At that he laughed heartily. Of course he did. "Civilization is not getting your bar mirror shot out," he explained.

"I see. Mr. Slocum, may I borrow your glass of water?"

"My pleasure."

Like its predecessor, this glass emptied on MacArdle's shirt front. MacArdle blanched. What this woman was doing was reminiscent of what her husband used to do to him. Rich with offended dignity, he wiped off his shirt front with the bar towel. He was distressed when he caught the young whore's eyes. Maybe it was violence that excited her, not him. He smiled an apology and hurried away down the bar, where a number of empty glasses waited for attention.

"Hey, you son of a bitch." That was Mother Sue's cry. Both her breasts were out of her bodice now and flopping around like an old mare's dugs. The Yellow Kid had one hand up her skirt and had hold of the prize, and she was smacking his grinning face weakly with her pudgy little fists.

"Oh come on now, Sue," her swain protested without releasing his trophy.

"You're hurting me, damn it."

Bonnie Slade turned to Slocum and said, "I don't believe Mr. MacArdle will be able to create his new civilization on such foundations as Virginia City provides."

"Likely not," Slocum agreed, grinning.

"Now, you turn me loose, Kid," said Mother Sue. "If you want some fun, you know where to find me."

"I already found you, Sue."

"Damn you. Damn you."

MacArdle's voice: "If you ladies can't behave yourselves, you'll have to take your business elsewhere."

The tenderfoot's eyes were big as four-bit pieces. One or two of the hardcases around the table had the tenderfoot marked as prey and hoped that he'd decided to take a little ride around the territory, preferably somewhere pretty far from Virginia City, where the damn vigilantes were so strong. One man, a fine-featured tall man with a warm twinkle in his eye, had already suggested a little late-season hunting party for the dude in the Crazy Mountains, where the biggest elk were and where two men could enjoy the serenity and solitude nature provided.

Sure, the dude said. Why not?

A couple of men came up to Mrs. Slade to say how sorry they were about her husband and ask whether there was anything they could do. Bonnie Slade looked at both of them as though they were trying a con game on her that was beneath her intelligence.

She discouraged what could have become a parade of insincerity.

MacArdle continued to find the other end of the bar more interesting than this one. She called to him again. "MacArdle. Another drink."

He looked up from polishing his glasses. He showed his teeth in what might pass for a smile and motioned for one of his bartenders to take care of the lady.

When the drink and glass were in front of her, she called again. "MacArdle, I said that I want a goddamn drink, and I don't see one here before me."

MacArdle's stomach had turned sour ever since the Slade woman had started in on him, and he was in no mood for trifling. Although the young whore had abandoned the other end of the bar to sit near him, MacArdle had lost most of his interest; even her lascivious smile didn't sway him.

Mother Sue's swain had his arm under her full skirts. Although it wasn't possible to see what he was doing, her face was happy as a full moon in October, and her eyes were shut. The sweat cut gullies in her makeup and uncovered old smallpox scars.

With all the flexibility of a steel ramrod, MacArdle stalked back down the bar. He had no temper left. First her husband and now this. He didn't care what the town thought. Bonnie Slade was as much a trollop as these other women. When he was done, not one of them would ever dare show her face in any establishment belonging to Jacob MacArdle.

He turned with the mechanical regularity of a parade-ground soldier. Promptly, she sloshed his shirt with her glass of water. She waited a bit before she tossed the shotglass of whiskey into his eyes.

"About time you took a bath," somebody shouted. "What's it been, MacArdle? Six months?"

The whiskey stung his eyes, and he was reaching behind himself for a bar towel, half blinded. He knocked a full bottle of rye whiskey onto the duckboards, where it shattered, which did not improve his temper.

His face was white with anger. "Mrs. Slade," he began ominously.

She dug into her reticule, and he actually thought that she had something more in there to throw at his shirt. He made a grab for her wrist but missed and found himself eye to eye with a Remington Double Action revolver.

"Oh, my God," he said.

The surprise was so great, the pistol so unlike what MacArdle had expected, that, just briefly, he lost control of himself, and a little dribble of pee stained his underclothes.

"My husband owned these pistols," Bonnie Slade said.

Nobody moved. Nobody in MacArdle's risked a breath, except for Mother Sue and her swain. Both of them had their eyes closed as his hand sent her into the throes of pleasure. Her mouth was open, and she was gasping like a trout on a sandbar.

One of her girls giggled, and the giggle was almost as loud as Mother Sue's gasps.

The sweat was running down MacArdle's forehead. Very carefully, he set the heels of his hands on the bar, jarring nothing, offering no threat. His underclothes were damp, and he hoped that the stain wouldn't show.

Mother Sue said, "Oh, honey. Honey."

Bonnie Slade cocked the Remington, and the clicking of the hammer stole Mother Sue's orgasm from her. At the familiar sound, her eyes flew open. Her head jerked even as her hand grabbed her sweetheart's wrist and held it still. Her face was wet. Her hair was wet at the hairline. The Yellow Kid hadn't heard the sound and wanted to keep on with her, but her grip on his wrist was tough as an iron brake band, and he couldn't do anything but retreat from his slippery, wet prize. The Yellow Kid wiped his hand on her skirts. She closed her knees and shook her breasts back into her dress.

Jack's Remington had a hump below the hammer and a shorter barrel than most Colts. The trigger guard was larger and the hammer spur smaller. Jack Slade owned two, both nickel-plated so that they wouldn't rust.

Bonnie Slade laid the second pistol between MacArdle's hands. She turned the butt so that it would be convenient for his grasp. "Who did Jack Slade murder, Mr. MacArdle?" she asked in a voice that contained equal measures of deadly reasonableness and grief.

"Your husband—"

"Who did my husband rob, Mr. MacArdle? My

husband was a rough man, and I suspect that many would shun his company, but I do not know who he killed."

"Ma'am," MacArdle said hoarsely.

"Who?"

"Well, I never heard that your husband killed anybody in Virginia City."

"That confirms what I had already known, Mr. Mac-Ardle, and I thank you for the confirmation." She had a funny way of talking, like the self-taught who've never heard spoken words they know well from reading alone. "Then my husband was a road agent? He held up travelers on the road and stole their possessions?"

It was easier now that MacArdle knew what she wanted. "No, ma'am, he never. . . ."

"Never was a road agent."

"No, ma'am. It wasn't that at all. What he did was shoot up my saloon." That was as sure a truth as had been spoken that day, but it wasn't what MacArdle had meant to say. He'd meant to say something about property rights or how a man should be able to go about his business without fear.

She smiled at his answer, which wasn't funny. She lifted the pistol with both hands, squinting along its barrel unsteadily. The crowd at the far end made room. Mother Sue got dumped on the floor, and the Yellow Kid tried to wiggle underneath her. Those who could get behind the protection of the bar did so, and those who couldn't, lay as flat as playing cards.

Lillie Langtry's full-length portrait loomed through the smoke. The pistol wavered from side to side.

X. Beidler came in the front, although only Slocum saw him. Beidler's eyes were bright as a diamond and nearly as hard.

The pistol barked, and the picture Jack Slade shot up so often had a new hole put there by his wife.

"There," Bonnie Slade said with some satisfaction. "Now I suppose you'll be wanting to hang me, too."

"No, ma'am," MacArdle said. He was tired of this farce and started to lift his hands, but she pushed the pistol at his face, and he replaced them. "No, ma'am. We don't hang a woman for that."

"Well, that's what you hanged my husband for."

"No, ma'am. Your husband was a dangerous man. Sooner or later he was going to do some real harm."

"So you did harm to him?"

MacArdle's stomach hurt like the dickens. He wanted to go home. He wanted to get out of his underclothes and wash himself. He wanted to put his head under the pillow. He kept still.

"You murdered him, Mr. MacArdle. You accused him as I accuse you. It was dreadful murder that you did this afternoon, and you'll roast in hell for it."

She lowered her pistol to her side. She nodded at the pistol that lay beside his hand. She said, "Fill your hand, you son of a bitch."

Slocum said, "Bonnie. . . ."

MacArdle said, "Mrs. Slade."

She said, "I'll count to three. One, two, three."

MacArdle gave her a knowing smile, which lasted until the bullet snapped his head back and slammed him into his own mound of polished glassware. His arm shot out, and he pulled a whole row of glasses down to the duckboards with him. His feet beat the duckboards like a dancer's.

Bonnie Slade lowered her husband's pistol. She said, "That's justice."

"No, ma'am. That ain't justice. I'm justice." The little figure materialized at her elbow. "X. Beidler, ma'am. At your service. I was able to provide help to your husband this afternoon, and it looks like I'll be providing some help for you."

6

"She went too far," X. Beidler argued stubbornly. "Just like that damn scoundrel husband of hers. They're birds of a feather. Out of the same nest, by God."

"Mr. Beidler," Judge Batesworth interjected, "Bonnie Slade is a woman."

"I thought she was a woman first time I laid eyes on her," Beidler said dryly. He fired up a cigar, and for a moment the only sound in the little downstairs room at the back of the Fairweather Inn was Beidler drawing on his smoke. One of the committee men went over to the sideboard, where a few bottles of whiskey and some glasses held down a tray. Carefully he poured himself a modest shot. No sense getting known as a boozer in this company.

Twelve men constituted the heart of the Committee of Vigilance. Although everyone knew that Batesworth and Beidler were at the heart of the business, no other list would have included all the other ten, although nobody would have missed them all, either. They were professionals, mostly, although two were small miners. They were more educated than the general rule, although one of them signed his name with a mark. They were concerned about the town, and the Vigilance Committee was the only way of showing their concern. That's what they had in common. Later, they'd form a fire company. Later, there'd be a school for the children. Later on, there'd be a courthouse and a law officer and a law more various than the law of Colonel Colt. That's what the Committee of Vigilance was: the first tentative steps toward civilization.

They'd been in on it from the beginning, from the day they'd hanged Plummer's two deputies. There wasn't a man in there who hadn't dragged on the working end of a rope, and there wasn't a pair of ears that hadn't heard the terrible croupy choking of a strangling man. They were in on it, a little over their heads, and there were some who would have thrown the vigilantes over in a minute if the federal government would just send a marshal or two into this part of the territory as they'd promised.

X. Beidler wasn't sick of it. He'd found his life's work, and it suited him down to his black, high-topped shoes, which were polished fresh every morning, no matter that they had to be washed free of mud and horseshit every night before he lay down.

X. Beidler always dressed well. It was one of his distinctions. Once upon a time he'd carried a shotgun with a tremendously long barrel, much longer than he was, but he'd given that up because a shotgun was a teamster's weapon, a blacksmith's choice, a ruffian's instrument. He never thought that he'd become a gentleman, but he moved among the gents and had to dress for the occasion. He carried two short-barreled Colts in his belt. They'd started out life as ordinary Colt .44's, pocket pistols, but Beidler had gone to work on them. He cut the front of the trigger guard away and shortened the barrel from four to two inches. He'd filed off the front sight and replaced the long hammer with a shorter, fatter spur. He created a belly gun. It wasn't a bit of use outside the length of the average barroom, but inside there wasn't anything faster.

"We shouldn't have hanged Jack Slade," Judge Batesworth said. He used the word "we" because he was a gentleman. He didn't remind anyone that he'd been against the hanging from the first.

"He'd gone too far," Beidler snapped.

Done was done. What did the hanging this morning have to do with the hanging tomorrow morning? They'd need a new rope, that was all. Someone who'd been in the Vigilance Committee out in San Francisco told a horror story of a rope that had been used so hard that one day it broke, leaving a man who'd already commended his soul to God standing on the scaffold with the rope dangling down his chest like a real necktie and the most awful look of surprise on his face. It's hard to hang a man once, harder to hang him twice. The Vigilance Committee used brand-new ropes. It got so that people cut them into short pieces as soon as they cut down the executed party and kept the short pieces as souvenirs. One half-wit who lived up behind the mercantile was said to have a collection of twenty rope pieces.

"You can't let anyone in the community go too far," Beidler said, setting his lips hard. "Now, that Slade was a real bad hat. I knew it"—he pointed his stubby finger —"you knew it, and I'll be damned if he didn't know it, too. If he hadn't murdered someone here, he surely had elsewhere, and he'd have done it here, too, given half a chance. What satisfaction would it have been to a dead citizen's kin to know their Vigilance Committee had its eye on the man who'd killed their kinsman? You tell me that. We didn't take a life this morning. We saved several innocent ones, and I, for one, have had my last word on the matter of Jack Slade and ain't going to say more about it."

"Dead is dead," Judge Batesworth said softly.

Beidler gave him a funny look but didn't reply.

The business at hand was unpleasant, and nobody

wanted to get on with it. Batesworth favored sending
Bonnie Slade out of the territory, maybe back to Utah,
where she'd come from. Beidler was all for hanging her.

"It don't matter what someone has between their
legs," he said. "Women can kill just as easy as a man,
and they can hang for it, too, just like a man."

The others weren't so sure. "She was awful damn
provoked," one said.

"Provoked? Of course she was provoked. Every day,
one or the other of us gets provoked. Hell, I'm provoked
right now." Beidler had a habit of jumping to his feet for
one of his speeches and then settling back into a chair,
deaf, dumb, and still. Sitting next to him was like sitting
next to a jack-in-the-box. It made a man nervous.

"Well, MacArdle was her husband's accuser."

"Of course he was. If there'd been a few more men in
town with guts, Jack Slade would have had a few more
accusers." Beidler sat down.

Batesworth said, "Damn, Beidler, will you stop jumping up like that? Every time you come out of that chair, I
swear I fear you're going to knock me down."

There was laughter, some of it nervous.

"Well," another man observed, "we can't keep a
woman prisoner."

One suggested that they cut off all her hair, strip her
naked, and tar and feather her and leave her on the
outskirts after marching her out of town on a rail. He
said that he'd seen that done once to a whore in Indiana.
It had made quite a spectacle. It sounded like he'd
enjoyed the spectacle.

"I've had that woman in my office. I've listened to her
acquire the rudiments of an education. I've tutored that
girl. She's an upright, intelligent woman with more
spunk than most men in these parts," Batesworth said.

"Yeah. Ask Jacob MacArdle about her spunk. He can
give her a fine reference." Beidler spoke dryly.

"Well, what are we going to do?" someone asked. "Jesus, it's getting late, and I've got an overland coach going out at dawn tomorrow."

"It's just midnight."

"Where did you say you had the girl?"

"That woman. Woman, Judge." Beidler made it sound like a woman was a very bad thing indeed.

"Mr. Beidler, this day has surely tried us all. Let's not try each other now." Judge Batesworth's raised eyebrows barely concealed his rising temper.

"She's down in the stable."

"But surely that's no place—"

"For a murderess?" Beidler's eyebrows were just as high as the judge's, and he was almost as angry. "I never thought a human being who'd shoot another in cold blood deserved a palace to sleep in."

Batesworth turned away. He poured himself a long drink, because it was going to have to be a long night if he wasn't to see Bonnie Slade hang.

Beidler had marched her over to the stable room first fitted out by Henry Plummer five years ago and used by hundreds of drunks and other prisoners since then. Since there was no privy attached, the horse stalls smelled better, and since there were no windows, the horses got better light, too.

Bonnie Slade hadn't been eager to go into that black stinking room, but Beidler had hold of her elbow. She asked for and got a fresh layer of straw tossed in on top of the droppings of the prisoners who'd gone before. They pushed her inside, and she sat down with her back to the wall.

It was dead black, black as the hell to which she thought herself consigned. She had meant to shoot MacArdle, no question about that. Her head shook in vigorous affirmation. There could be no mistake about it. She had given him his chance to fight fair and square, and one chance was all he had deserved. Now she deserved whatever she was going to get. She hoped they would hang her, because Judge Batesworth's whisper to her that maybe they'd send her back to Utah held more terrors than the hangman's rope.

The planks weren't quite as tight-fitting as they'd first appeared, and there was plenty of moonlight streaming into the interior of the stable, some of which reflected off the walls and outlined every plank with its own gray outline. The outside walls and ceiling were doubled, and she could sense them only with her fingertips. The cracks in the front wall of her jail were just wide enough to see through, but not so wide that you could pass anything in or out.

Satisfied with her examination, though not with its results, she sat again and asked herself what an educated woman would have done if her husband had been hanged. She noted that Lady Macbeth and Medea had been fairly fierce, but they were probably exceptions to the general run of heroines. She tried to think of a heroine who'd killed her husband's murderer but couldn't remember one. Most of the heroines were weak-willed. They could kill themselves, all right, or even their children, like Medea, but they couldn't kill a fool like Jacob MacArdle.

The stable room smelled awful. She would have gagged, but once she started, the smell of her own vomit would start a process she couldn't stop. Best to stop before it got started. For a moment she pinched her nostrils. She wasn't accustomed to breathing through her mouth and could almost taste the odor she could no longer smell. She ran her other hand through her long hair and was pleased that it hadn't got too mussed. If she'd been standing directly in front of MacArdle, she might have gotten splattered with his blood, but she'd been far back enough to be spared that messy excess. She smiled. MacArdle had been very surprised.

John Slocum was in the Bullwhacker, working on a monumental drunk. He'd swallowed half a bottle of the Bullwhacker's finest, but that hadn't helped a bit. His sight was slightly blurry at the edges, but his brain was still racing a mile a minute. The Yellow Kid sat beside him at the bar, having reopened shop for the occasion. The big crowd was at MacArdle's. The sounds across the street came in two sizes: hilarity and solemnity. One built toward the other and then went back again. For about half an hour MacArdle's would be quiet as a tomb, and then the horseplay would start again. Men enjoyed MacArdle's death in a way they'd never really enjoyed MacArdle, and there were more men concerned with where they'd been when they heard the shot than ever had been interested in talking to him or asking his opinions. In death, he was famous for a night.

The Yellow Kid had some of the instincts of a vulture, which is to say that he always had his eye out for a free meal, and often as not, that meal required that somebody else do something. He had finished off less whiskey than John Slocum but was quite a bit drunker.

"How about that Bonnie Slade." He chuckled. "When she laid that damn Remington on the bar, I thought MacArdle would croak on the spot. And then challenging him like that. That little girl's got more nerve in her little finger. . . ."

"All nerve, no brains." Slocum sighed.

"You mean you think old MacArdle didn't deserve it?"

"Of course he did. Jacob MacArdle should have been strangled at the teat. Would have saved the world a passel of trouble. Hell, do you think anybody in town is sorry he's gone?"

"Maybe Bonnie Slade. Maybe she's having second thoughts."

"Oh, hell." Slocum poured another drink. He didn't really want it, but he drank it, anyway.

"She sure is a looker, that one. Ain't hard to see what Jack Slade saw in her."

"She's handsome, that's true."

"I wonder if they'll string her up. Necktie party seems like such a waste." The Yellow Kid poured himself a drink. He didn't want the whiskey any more than Slocum did, but couldn't resist a free one.

"Oh, hell, they won't hang her. Never been a woman hanged in the territory."

"First time for everything. Yes, sir, there's a first time for everything. If old Beidler gets his way, she'll swing, that's certain. The committee's meetin' right now at the Fairweather."

"Yeah?"

"Don't you think of speakin' for her," the Yellow Kid said, waggling his finger. "She's got plenty of trouble without you helpin' her out. Christ, with Jack Slade gone, you're the roughest cob in Virginia City. They'll be lookin' at you next."

Slocum was remembering a run-in he'd had years ago with Beidler. Beidler and Slocum had both been younger then. Beidler was harder now. Slocum wondered whether he was harder, too.

"What about that Bonnie Slade?" The Yellow Kid was admiring her again.

"Jesus, you're boring. Don't you know any jokes?"

With that, John Slocum walked out of the Bullwhacker, leaving the remnants of the whiskey bottle behind him. He was as sober as when he had come, and he walked with the grace of a highly tuned animal.

A thought crossed the Yellow Kid's bleary mind: Here goes trouble.

* * *

Judge Batesworth was in his sixties. X. Beidler wasn't thirty-five. Batesworth wanted Bonnie Slade exiled from the territory for her crime, and Beidler wanted her hanged. Most of the other vigilantes were in the middle about it. X. Beidler looked at the judge's weary old eyes and thought: I'll hang her in the morning. You'll be dead to the world by then, and she'll just be dead.

Bonnie Slade pressed herself up to the gray lines that outlined the planks of her prison wall. Most of them were so close together that all she could see was light and shadow. Through one of them she could make out one —no, two—figures sitting on the ground, backs against the stall facing her. One of the figures lit a smoke, a young man, a miner from the look of him. She saw that in the light of a match that seemed to her as bright as a rising sun.

His companion said something, and Bonnie pressed her ear against the wall. She could hear or see, but not both at once.

"Christ almighty, pal. Don't you know better than to smoke in here? In a stable full of straw? It could go up in a minute, and then where'd we be?"

The other guard mumbled something low and rough, but Bonnie couldn't make out the words. It was uncomfortable with her ear pressed to the wall, but at least it helped her forget the stink of the place. She stayed on her heels. Despite the layer of straw they'd forked over the old bedding, she wouldn't sit down, not until her ankles wouldn't hold her up anymore.

She thought about John Slocum. He was a lot like Jack Slade in his loyalty to his friends and his quick, rough temper. But Slocum had learned to read somewhere, and he knew some of what pleased a woman. There was a tiny glow deep in her breast from thinking of him, a glow like a small furnace. Thinking of him warmed her, when she hadn't known she was chilled. She wondered whether she'd ever miss Jack and decided no. She'd buried him when she killed MacArdle. Puffy little MacArdle, so self-important. It was funny, but she felt like her bullet had, for one instant, shown him the real world and then plunged him into darkness.

What was she to do? She was all alone. Alone by choice, but alone. She made an inventory of her strengths. She had perhaps $50 worth of household goods at the soddy, and she owned Jack's saddle horse, which was worth maybe another $50. His guns would fetch almost as much, but they'd taken them away from her, and she didn't expect to see them again. She had a slight friendship with one man, John Slocum, and one vigilante, Judge Batesworth. She could read and write and had read more than most adult males of her acquaintance. She was—she considered it objectively—very good-looking, although she wouldn't wear so well as women with better bones than hers.

Once again she pressed her eye to the crack in the boards. One of the guards had settled down, but the smoker was still wide awake. It would cost his life to let her out of here. The vigilantes would think he'd been bought off. If she had enough money, she would buy him off, but she hadn't. She did have her body. She pulled back from the crack in the boards and thought for a long moment. In her life, three men had had her, two of them more often than Jack Slade, because Jack was drunk so often that he usually had no interest. She was indifferent. She insisted that they wait until she was wet before they plunged into her, but that was her only wish. Sometimes, afterward, she felt a warm glow of affection. This affection she had felt for the last two of the three men, and she would feel it, she was sure, for any man she should happen to sleep with regularly. More than that, no.

What did she want? She didn't really want another man. She and Jack Slade were square now, since she'd killed his murderer, and she had no great desire to take on another set of obligations. She didn't want to become a whore, although she suspected that she'd be good at it. Last night, Mother Sue had horrified her. She wouldn't want to be Mother Sue, not if she died for not being like that. She wondered what time it was. When she pressed her eye to the crack in the boards again, her guard had put out his smoke but was still sitting in the same place. It must be after midnight. She didn't want to hang, but the thought held few terrors for her. There were worse things than being hanged. Being degraded was one of them, and being a prisoner was another.

A wave of sadness came over Bonnie Slade. The unfairness made her mad. She was twenty-three years old, had left one husband, and had lost another to hanging. She'd been prepared only for a life she'd grown to hate enough to flee with the first passing stranger. But she'd been lucky. Slocum's little gift of two books had sparked more in her than she would have guessed possible. Bonnie Slade had wishes where before she'd had only daydreams. Once she'd daydreamed about living on a far-off island, naked all the time. She'd filled her days with such foolishness. Now she thought about buying a steamer ticket to the Pacific islands. She wondered how much it might cost and how she could earn the money. She liked her life, she liked her thoughts, and she liked what had been her dreams and now were her plans.

It would be awful to die here and now. She honestly believed that if someone had come to the Mormon stage station where she'd been so miserable and offered to hang her, she might have taken up the offer, her life was so hopeless and her heart so dead. But not now. For God's sake, not now. She was banging on the door of her prison before she realized what she was doing.

"Ma'am? Ma'am? You'll have to quit that now. Ma'am? Is anything wrong?"

She doubled up her fist and put her knuckles in her mouth so that she wouldn't scream. There was nothing wrong that a rope with thirteen knots wouldn't cure. She bit down, bit deep.

"Ma'am? I hope you're all right in there. I hope nothing's gone bad for you."

His voice was young, not much more than a kid's. Bonnie Slade heard the uncertainty in his voice, and a kind of glee possessed her for a moment. Maybe, if she could just figure how to do it, this might be her reprieve. She clamped her jaws tight, just in case she had another scream that might try to get out. She rapped sharply on the door three times and then three times again.

"Ma'am? I sure hope you're not sick in there. I surely wish they had put a little window in this here door, but I guess they never thought of it."

She held her hand back and waited. Every bit of her strained to hear and understand the life at the other side of the door. Suddenly, she slipped down to her knees in the straw so that she could peer through the crevice and see who or what was on the other side: heavy twelve-ounce denims, almost brand-new, and stiff, a pair of worn-out miner's boots with brown spliced laces. The legs belonged to the young voice.

"Ma'am?"

She reached above her own head and pounded then, pounded like something desperate, like someone desperate, like desperation itself. She pounded until her ears were filled with blood and roaring. When she dropped her fist, it was sore, and she wondered whether she'd broken a bone, right there at the edge of the hand that had taken the brunt of the pounding.

"Ma'am. Speak to me. Please speak to me."

The boy's voice cracked then and climbed into the childhood register. The sweat ran down Bonnie's face, not from the work of the pounding but from the work of willing the boy to open the door.

She heard a rattle and scuttled back deeper into the cell until her back was against the far wall; she was suddenly frightened of what she had conjured up. She'd been in the converted stable just three hours, and already it had assumed comforting airs. It was her lair, and someone was letting the light into it.

He swung the heavy wooden door open. The moon-light was so bright that the guard was just a shadow in a bright rectangle with no depth or dimensions. He couldn't see her at all.

"Ma'am? Ma'am? You sick? You want me to call my father?"

She knew the voice, although she didn't know where she'd heard it before. It was very important that she remember where she'd heard this adolescent voice. She could smell something. His voice reminded her of a smell, the smell of damp laundry—no, damp pages before a fire.

"I'm Robert Batesworth, ma'am. I expect you don't remember me."

She did: the little room where she'd reported on her reading, the cover of the book sometimes damp from the snow, and Judge Batesworth looking at her with his kindly eyes. Surely she remembered his son. But he was just a boy. How did she happen to be guarded by a boy?

"I must come out, Robert," she said softly. She put kindliness in her voice.

He would find some excuse to pass through the room where she'd studied, and a time or two she'd caught him gazing at her, moonstruck as a calf. He covered his hair with grease and parted it clean. She doubted that the judge ever noticed his son much. He was very old, and the boy was very young, and the boy's mother was dead.

"Robert, I must come out."

The boy looked around nervously. "I can't, Mrs. Slade. My father sent me here to keep a guard over you until morning. And Mr. Beidler, he sent Beamis over here, but Beamis had a bottle of whiskey and said I should take the first watch. Are you all right?" By now his eyes had adjusted to the dark. He took half a step inside the cell. "Ma'am?"

"I can't breathe, Robert. Before God, I can't breathe."

"Well, I'd catch the dickens if I was to let you outside."

"Two strong men? What could I do against two strong men. Robert, I saw my husband hanged this noon."

He bowed his head. He was very young. "Yes, ma'am."

She made a horrible sound like the choking sound Jack Slade had made.

Bonnie Slade didn't have any firm ideas about escape. Outside, in the wider confines of the livery, she was farther from the noose than she was when inside that stinking converted tack room. That was all she knew.

The sound scared the life out of the boy. Despite himself, he put one hand to his mouth.

She didn't ask again but just headed right for him. If he wasn't to smash her with the closing door, he had to let her out, which he did, stepping aside at the very last moment. She felt his breath as she passed.

She'd made a fair amount of ruckus in the last half hour. Beamis, X. Beidler's man, rolled half onto his side, curled his legs up, put his arms between his legs, and snored greatly.

She walked just like a convict after chains have been

cut, although she hadn't worn chains at all. It was the freedom that made her weak. She knew that she had to reassure the boy, because he would put her right back in there if he got scared enough. She sat down where he'd been sitting, and, putting her head back, she breathed in great draughts of air that smelled faintly of horses and hay.

The boy closed the door behind him, because the stench was appalling, worse than he'd thought, and he wanted to keep the stink confined. He'd known the woman he guarded before. To him, she had always seemed like an innocent victim of Jack Slade. Her beauty caused a few stains on the boy's bedclothes when his imagination conjured her. The boy had a tremendous urge to protect this woman, an urge he'd never spoken of to his father. His father had given him this duty because Robert was sixteen years old now, and it was time he took on some of the responsibilities of a man.

Her eyes were closed; her head was back. He longed to hold her and comfort her; but he was the guard, and she was the prisoner.

Like most young men, he was an ironist. While he spent his lonely hours outside the door of her cell, he had been thinking of her, thinking how bitter it was that he should be so in love with the prisoner he was guarding. This thought pleased him with its ironic twist, and he'd entertained himself with that and other morose notions. The moonlight, to him, was the white color of a winding sheet, and, of course, he saw the stars as cold and indifferent.

She wasn't going to go anywhere; he could see that. He said, "I'd get you a drink of water, but I can't leave you alone."

"That's all right." Her lips were parched, but she didn't want to make him say no. "Thank you. I was going to die in there."

He misunderstood. "You ain't going to die," he said fiercely. "They've never hung a woman in the territory." His fists were clenched as though they might keep the territory's record unblemished. They unclenched when he added, "My father is rooting for you. He took quite a shine to you."

"He's a fine man." There was weariness in her voice. "A fine man."

"Well, he likes you a lot. Ever since Ma died, he's been alone. He ain't going to let anything happen to you."

She raised her fine blue eyes to his. "How about you, Robert? Will you help me?"

His eyes went away, and with all her fierce will she wanted them back again. His eyes ducked and dodged like rabbits ahead of the dogs, but they returned to her and the dreadful question. The boy decided to become a man. "No," he said. "I ain't going to let them hang you."

He stood a little straighter. His voice didn't crack at all, but his own words went bouncing around the cavern of his brain and scared him a little. He would have taken them back if he could have.

She patted the ground next to her. He hastened to occupy the space.

"Thank you for letting me out. That air would have killed me before morning."

"It sure smells horrible. I don't know how they'd think to put a lady in there."

"That was Beidler's doing." She made that name an ugly word.

"Yes. Say, I don't know. Does he have some sort of grudge against you?"

"He's just one of those men who can't stand anything that isn't smooth and perfectly even. If he had his way, everything would be perfectly square and chained in place: square trees, square horses, square men, and square women. He hates, Robert. He's a man who hates."

He didn't half understand her, but she'd put her hand over his while she was talking and forgotten to remove it. He didn't suggest that she do so, and he didn't want to say anything that might remind her.

Bonnie Slade hadn't spotted the sleeping man's weapons, although she supposed that he had a pistol tucked in the straw somewhere near. The boy had an Army Colt in the holster his father had worn in the war. The holster was fastened neatly shut with a snap at the top, and he wore it on his left hip.

She heard a couple of horses walk by outside and didn't say anything, because she didn't want anyone to hear her voice. The horses stopped for the longest time, but then they went on, and she didn't hear them anymore. Her hand was sweaty, and she hoped that the boy didn't notice it or notice how hard her heart was pounding. She wondered how many horses were in the stalls and which was the fastest.

The boy's hand was wet with sweat, too, but he didn't move it because he was afraid that she'd notice where her hand was.

She choked slightly. Her throat narrowed down to the tinest hole, but she said, "I don't know what I'll do without Jack. I'm so alone."

He dared it. He gave her soft hand a squeeze. "Oh, hell, Bonnie, there's plenty of fellows would give a lot just to be with you and take care of you." He laughed. "You don't have to worry about being lonely."

She was worried about being hanged. Lonely didn't worry her a bit. "Who could care for me now that I've killed a man? Oh, Robert, I was so frightened."

He nodded stoutly. "He had a gun, too. If he'd elected to try for it, I don't believe you'd be sitting here now, ma'am. You offered him a chance."

This last speech was one Robert had rehearsed during the hours he'd guarded Bonnie. Damn, he felt lucky. He felt like everything was going to work out all right. He wished that he didn't have pimples on his face, but it was dark, too dark for her to see them.

Beamis, Beidler's man, snored. There was some noise behind the stable.

"Do you know what time it is?" she whispered.

"About three, I reckon."

"When they hang people, they hang them at dawn, don't they?"

He didn't want to answer that question. He knew that she knew her hand was in his, and she'd chosen to leave it there.

"I don't want to be hanged, Robert."

Loyally, he said something about his father's preventing any such catastrophe, but he didn't know any better than she did what her fate was to be. He did know that her free hand was touching his neck now, right at the hollow.

"If I do have to die," she said softly, "I want it to be beautiful." Instinctively, she touched the heart of the young romantic. It was just about where she'd thought it would be.

When she kissed him, she sealed their romantic bargain. She kissed him like someone who was hungry for life, and the boy, who had known only brief kisses snatched amid gigglings, was terrified. Her lips found his, like a snake trying to eat its prey. Her tongue pursued his no matter where he put it, and he couldn't escape.

He thought: She's a married woman. She's done *everything* before. And that brought him out of his terror. Somewhat tentatively, he kissed her back. She was laying half across him now, with her knee between his, and he was getting very hard down there. His hands were on her shoulders, because he was afraid that he'd misread the signals, afraid of what it meant, afraid of what she wanted.

"I won't hurt you," she said very softly and with a little mischief in her voice.

He coughed into his hand. Gruffly, he said, "Maybe we should find a nice clean stall. We wouldn't want him to wake up."

"No, we wouldn't." There was a note of pure amusement in her voice.

Again he coughed. When he stood up, he half turned away because he didn't want her to see the bulge in the front of his almost-new pants.

"It looks nice in here," she said. It was a large stall, clean underneath, with a good bedding of oat straw on top. There was light to see, and they left the front door of the stall open to let the moonlight in. She stood at the end of the stall like an offering or a doe in the field. There was no fear in her eyes, only something like mocking humor.

She wore a simple gingham dress with the buttons down the front, and now her fingers went to the top button and unfastened it. Her throat was soft in the moonlight. The boy caught his breath. He was afraid to move lest he fumble.

"Come over here," she said. Her voice was soft as a kitten in the cream.

He stepped toward her.

"Aren't you going to take off your boots?" That same mocking humor.

He propped his butt against the stall to remove his miners' boots. His socks had holes in the bottoms, and so he wadded them up and stuffed them into his boot tops.

"The young judge, that's who you are. Let me help you with that sleeve." Her hand brushed his holster as she tugged his shirt out of his trousers, but he was too lost in her kisses to notice it, and he didn't notice anything different about the holster once the flap was unfastened.

"My young judge. My young judge."

His hands were at her full breasts, his thumbs wondering at her nipples, tracing them.

"Relax, young judge. Relax now. We have a long time ahead of us."

Her words almost made him come in his pants, and her knee was in between his, rubbing him with soft strokes. Her bare skin was against his groin. His hands reached around behind her, and he felt the fabric of her dress sliding around, slippery as new-cut grass, over her bare skin.

His hands tried one of the buttons, the button at her waist. He'd never undressed anyone before, and his hands couldn't work the button, but she stayed still for his fumbling until she knew that his impatient fingers were about to pop the button.

"Don't tear it," she whispered. Her fingers fluttered, and the gate was opened.

The dark junction between her thighs. He brushed it first with the back of one hand, and that brief contact with her womanhood made the hair stand up on his arms.

"Take off your pants."

"Sure, Bonnie." They were the first words he'd spoken, and they were not a child's and not a man's.

She felt an immense and sudden sadness for him. But it wasn't enough, that sadness, not when they were going to hang her in the morning. She could almost love him, but the rope was in her mind, and her game was more complex than the complicated game of a man and a woman.

"Put your clothes over here. I'll sit on them so the straw won't cut up my . . . behind."

They both blushed at the word.

He tossed all his clothes on the straw except his boots. The gunbelt and his father's pistol and holster he set beside the boots. She moved the pile of clothes much closer to the stall door, within easy reach of where she'd be lying. He didn't notice a thing. His cock was hurting and poked toward her belly like it wanted to enter her navel. His arms were out. She sat up all of a sudden, her knees wide apart. He almost stumbled over her foot.

"Come to me, Robert," she crooned. "Inside of me."

His cock jerked, and he knew that he'd be lucky to get inside of her before he came, but he knelt just the same. He closed his eyes, with his trembling cock just above her belly and his head thrown back so that the neck muscles stood out. He was trying to think of something else, something to keep him from coming before he even got inside her. He was on the brink of the rush, just balanced.

Her hand groped down beside him, seeking the smooth leather of the holster. She had it, too, at the barrel end. Through the leather she could feel the projection of the Colt's front sight.

Her nose was burning. His eyes opened, and he looked at her, trying to understand something else besides love. "I smell smoke," he said, completely confused.

She sniffed. Her hand sought to turn the holster around without banging into his bare heel. "So do I."

"Smoke."

She had the holster by the flap now and was dragging it toward her a quarter inch at a time.

A sudden gust of wind, and it was unmistakable. He sneezed. Her eyes watered.

"My God," he said. "The damn stable's on fire."

The rear wall of the stable was aglow, as if the fire was outside but working itself in. The boy was coming now, spurting his seed all over her, but both of them were smelling the acrid smoke, and the boy's senses were so confused that he didn't know what he was doing. He reached for his pile of clothes, encountered her hand, and didn't think a thing of it. He didn't ask himself why her hand was there or what she was up to. He wanted to get his pants on. He'd never felt so exposed. He croaked the word "fire."

"It is. It's fire. We have to get out of here."

"Fire!" He yelled it so loud, it deafened her. Already he was hopping into his pants, and he had the holster tucked between his chin and his neck while he got into his clothes.

Bonnie Slade's fingertips itched. She almost snatched the holster. She'd heard a couple of horses out back, and it was bound to be dark outside, and she did know how to ride. She'd always known that.

"Fire," the boy screamed, and burst out of the stall, meaning to wake his sleeping partner.

Beamis, Beidler's man, was already sitting up, rubbing his eyes. "What the hell?"

"I told you that you shouldn't smoke in here!"

"That fire ain't here, kid, it's around back." Beamis noticed that much. He also noticed a figure slipping toward the front of the stable. "Hey!"

The kid whirled around. Beamis stood up. Bonnie ran for the front door, barefoot, her open dress sailing behind her like a bird's wings trying to get up enough speed to fly.

"Evenin', gents. Sorry about that fire. If you reach for your iron, you're dead."

John Slocum stepped into the open doorway just as Bonnie Slade hurtled past. Two good horses were at the hitch rack, the best horses you could buy in the middle of the night in Virginia City when money is no object.

Beamis said, "Damn." He was an old hand, and John Slocum's Colt was aimed somewhere between the two of them. They'd been caught square.

"We'll need a minute lead," Slocum said.

"God damn. X. Beidler will hunt you for this!"

"Well, you know how it is. Sometimes you run across a quarrel that won't let you alone until you take up with it."

Being that kind of old hand, Beamis left his pistol in his belt.

The boy was a disappointed lover and grabbed for his. His hand fumbled for the pistol butt, and when he had hold of it, he let the holster fall off the muzzle.

Slocum shot him low, because he was a kid. Even in the dim light, he could see that he was a kid. Beamis's hands flew up like a covey of quail. Beamis closed his eyes.

The bullet took the kid in the thick meat of the leg and turned him half around. He sat down. It didn't hurt. It was a blow like a horse kick. He'd felt worse. Sitting, he reached to kill the figure in the doorway. His barrel found a mark, and his thumb moved.

Beamis kicked him in the arm, and the pistol flew into the stall. The kid screamed with pain, because now it hurt.

Beamis kept his hands high.

"You would have killed him," Beamis explained.

"I didn't want to much," Slocum said, and eased his hammer down. He felt the trembling start at the back of his arm and along his whole shoulder, because it had been a near thing.

"You got your minute," Beamis said. "Thirty seconds is gone," he added.

"Be seein' you," Slocum said, and wheeled and ran for the horses.

7

The cold, misty sun found them riding on the banks of the Madison River, just south of Three Forks. The sun came up over the Big Belt Mountains and divided the shadow of the wide river valley, touching the opposite slopes of the divide with a glossy golden splendor.

"It's the divide up there," Slocum said, pointing at the western peaks fifty miles away.

Bonnie was tired. She hadn't laid her head down since the night before last, and the hours afterward had been full. "What divide?" she asked with asperity.

"The divide of the oceans," Slocum said. "If you stand on the very top of that range and spit just right, half of your spit will end up in the Atlantic and half will end up in the Pacific."

"That's nice to know."

The light on the high places made the valley darker. The low mist swirled around their horses' legs, and she shivered despite Slocum's heavy coat, which she had wrapped around herself. She asked, "Have you read about Alexander Bell's new discovery? A device that will enable us, one day, to talk through wires from one home to the next, even across continents."

"You ought to be glad that gadget isn't in use around

here. Old Beidler'd be speaking to every vigilance committee in the state."

She huffed. "I just think it's wonderful what progress is being made."

A couple of birds perched on a dead branch beside the river. They set up a wild calling as the two riders approached, and then they lifted off at the last minute. Black and red-orange plumage caught the light as the small birds darted away.

"That's a redstart," Slocum said.

"What?"

"The birds."

"What birds?"

"Over there. You can't see them now."

"Are you an ornithologist?"

"A what?"

"An ornithologist. A man who studies birds."

He shook his head.

She relented a little too late. "Well, I think it's just wonderful, all the things you know about the country-side. Did you come out here right after the war?"

Slocum hitched himself in the saddle so that a different patch of his ass would take the wear and tear. "Yeah."

"Well, so you see, sometimes war can have a benefi-cial result."

He was astonished. "What?"

She hadn't seen any of that country or that war. She'd been born in the West and had heard only horrible tales, tales leavened with the self-congratulation the Mormons were wont to feel for keeping out of it. She wasn't as hard as she sounded; she just didn't know better.

She chattered on. "All the sciences were advanced by discoveries made in armament design," she said, obliv-ious to his tight mouth and hardened eyes. Slocum had lost everything in that war.

The light lay on the top layers of low mist, and the

mist went pink at the touch, swirling about their horses' hooves so that it looked like they were riding through pink clouds.

Slocum's animal was a big standard-bred roan gelding. It was fast enough, and it seemed to be holding up pretty well on what was going to be a long ride, but he missed the Appaloosa's sure-footedness. He missed the Appaloosa.

"Lot of good came out of that war," he said. "Yes, sir."

She caught his sarcasm and shot him a glance. She opened her mouth to say something, thought better, and looked away. After a while, she said, "When do you think the railroad will come to the territory?"

Slocum grunted.

"Mr. Jim Hill has promised to put his Northern Pacific from coast to coast, from Chicago to Portland, Oregon."

"I reckon they'll put it through once all the Indians are dead. This country we're riding through used to belong to the Bannacks and the Crow. The Crow nation had a considerable number, but there weren't too many Bannacks. There's less now. Nothin' in them to worry about, though. Never brought harm to anybody. Just wander up and down this valley, huntin' and fishin'."

"It'll be a good thing when all the redskins are on reservations," she said.

He rolled his head around to get the cricks out of his neck. "Why's that?"

"Because civilization won't advance until they're all on reservations. A little exposure to civilization, that's all they need."

"Generally kills them," he remarked. "Look at the way that cottonwood's lyin' in the stream there. Now that's something you don't see too often. Plenty of trees get undercut into the stream, but not so many keep growin'."

The light caught at the dark green branches of the island cottonwood.

She rubbed her eyes. "The Indians," she continued, "are a constant danger."

He nodded. "Yep."

"And they should be put in civilized surroundings."

"Well," he said, "I've seen a few of the reservations. Some are hot, some are cold, some wet, some dry. They only got one thing in common. They're land nobody else wants. It isn't like the Indians were bein' sent to that Athens, Greece, you keep talking about. More like they're goin' to Andersonville or Yuma."

"Andersonville? Yuma?"

"Prisons, ma'am."

"Well, sometimes a few people have to give things up for the benefit of the rest."

"I'll be sorry to see them go. They were brave enemies and good friends, and they kept the spoilers east of the Missouri for a hundred years. That was their job, and they weren't so bad at it. Hell, the Sioux are still tearing up the prairie around the Missouri breaks. I heard they're sending General Crook out against them. Crook and Reno and George Armstrong Custer."

"Well, I hope they sweep the last of the Indians out of the way. Think of it, Mr. Slocum. The railroad."

She uttered the last two words with the awe normally reserved for a miracle or some other religious phenomenon.

"I suppose so," he said, inclined to cut the conversation short. The light was burning the mist now. His horse was steaming; his own shoulders were steaming. The heat felt good, and life was agreeable.

"Imagine the cities we'll build, the factories."

Slocum looked at the gorgeous spread of uninterrupted valley. Already on the Big Belts there was a light dusting of snow at the higher peaks, but it wasn't even full fall down here. The aspens along the river banks had all their leaves. An otter slipped into the river at their approach in that silent way they have, and the wake it left behind in the still water made it look like it was swimming through glistening oil.

"It will be so beautiful," she said.

"Yeah."

Across the banks, three antelope were lined up for a morning drink of water. Slocum and Bonnie came upon them so quickly that they were overpowered by curiosity and froze, like three statues in the water. The woman didn't see them until they broke and bounded into the deep buffalo grass.

She drew in her breath as the three animals bounded away. Then she said, "You love this country, don't you, Mr. Slocum?"

Slocum smiled. He'd never put it into words before, but he supposed he did. Why did he want to move on again, then? He supposed that he was just like one of the Sioux, forever on the move. "It's too good for the likes of us," he said softly. "Let's pull up over there where that sandy bottom is. The horses could use a drink, and my back end would sure enjoy a little respite."

"Do we dare?" She cast a glance at their back trail, marked clearly by the broken buffalo grass.

"Oh, I expect so. Old Beidler'll follow us sure, but I don't know whether he'll be able to get up much of a posse."

"For God's sake, Beidler, hasn't this gone far enough?" Judge Batesworth was talking, about five minutes after Slocum and Bonnie Slade had galloped out of town. The dust from their horses' hooves had barely settled on Main Street.

"We now have a matter of arson, Judge," Beidler said

softly. His voice sounded like that of a man rubbing his hands. "Arson and escaping from the authorities."

"Authorities?"

Beidler wasn't taken aback by the question. "Authorities," he repeated, placidly as a cow. "If the Vigilance Committee is not the authority, then Virginia City, no, the whole territory, ain't got one."

Batesworth's face was lit up on one side by the flames of the livery Slocum had fired. He stepped back a bit from the heat. The miners had gathered buckets, washtubs, hand basins, and even number-ten cans and were passing them along a line that stretched from Alder Creek to as close to the burning building as men could stand with wet shirts wrapped around their necks and wetted-down Stetsons to keep the embers out of their hair.

On the street side of the livery, other men were leading the last few terrified horses out of the inferno. The horses wore blinders or had clothes wrapped around their heads so that they couldn't see the danger. Still they screamed and whinnied. When a flaming ember touched the rump of the very last horse, it bolted, dropping its handler and hurtling up the street until it smashed right into the Virginia City Mercantile at the head of the street, right through its big front window with its mining tools and implements.

"What about your son, Judge?"

Beamis had dragged him outside before he started back after the horses. They had taken the boy up the street to Mother Sue's front parlor, where a sawbones said that his chances were good, that the bullet had gone clean through without touching bone, and rest would soon put him right.

The bucket brigade was sluicing down buildings on both sides of the livery, keeping the newspaper office wet, and on the other side the Virginia Reel café. They'd tired of throwing good water on the stable, and anyway, the roof was about to fall.

"The boy was hurt because of you, Beidler. You and me and that damned committee of experts. Expert fools, I'd call us. While we were arguing whether to murder a woman or not, my boy was getting shot."

Beidler said, "Seems to me, Judge, we was just about to let that woman go." He mocked the judge's own words. " 'She is a poor woman who should be exiled from Virginia City. She has done wrong only because we have wronged her.' We wronged her last night, Judge? Before she set fire to the livery and caused your boy to get shot?"

"Bonnie Slade is. . . . Oh, what's the use?" Dramatic as an actor, the judge threw one hand into the air and marched up the street. He had to be with his boy.

Beamis came up to his boss once the judge was away. Beamis didn't like Judge Batesworth and wasn't comfortable with him. "What did old Miss Batesworth want?" he asked. He spat a stream of tobacco at an ember lying on the street and extinguished it neatly.

Beidler had been pretty mad at Beamis, who, after all, was the adult member of the party set to guard the prisoner, but his anger at Batesworth was stronger.

"He doesn't want us to go after Slocum and the woman. He says he'll speak against forming a posse. He says we murdered Slade, and the woman is out of her head with grief. Batesworth is the enemy, Beamis. We'd best keep an eye on him. He means to do us harm."

Beidler folded his arms behind himself and watched the fire like a man watching a theatrical. Beamis put out his hands to warm them.

"Listen to that. Fire's really takin' off now."

"John Slocum's work, Beamis," Beidler said with some satisfaction. "Did I ever tell you about our previous meeting?"

Beamis knew that Beidler and Slocum had crossed paths once before, but Beidler had been curiously reluctant to comment on the matter. "No, boss."

"Blue Rock. Slocum was accused of murder. Another man did it. I followed him and nearly had him. When I learned Slocum was innocent, it broke my heart. I was much younger then."

Beamis cocked his head, waiting for more.

Beidler didn't disappoint him. "Yes, I was younger. Slocum is much like our friend Jack Slade. He doesn't have to do anything to be guilty. There's just some men that should be hanged for the sake of good order. I didn't know that then."

Beamis nodded eagerly. "He was the one freed the woman and fired the barn. He shot the boy and would've shot me, too, if I'd tried anything."

"Yes," said Beidler. "That would've been expecting too much of you, Beamis."

Beamis began to smile and then lost it. He nodded thoughtfully. "Too bad we can't chase Slocum as a horse thief," he said. "But he bought and paid for those two animals. Rousted their owner out of bed to do it, too."

"We've got enough. Maybe we'll get a trial where we capture him."

"After him?" Beamis had hoped for the rest of his bottle of whiskey and a bed for the remainder of the night.

"Get the horses."

Slocum and Bonnie Slade rode beside the Madison River until it became the Missouri at Three Forks, which was as far upstream as Lewis and Clark had followed the river before they left it and cut due west, hoping to reach the Pacific Ocean. That was in the fall of 1804, and they were the first whites in this part of the world. The buffalo grass was just like it had been eighty years ago, and the towhees nested in the rushes beside the river. The Madison had as many of the same big trout it had when Clark fished it.

They left the riverbank past Crow Mountain, a bare rock that floated above them like an Egyptian monument.

At noon they stopped for some beef jerky, but that was the only meal that day. As the weary horses climbed along the steep talus slopes, both riders were hungry.

"Jack Slade used to say that only a fool makes camp in the dark."

Slocum had a place spotted where he meant to camp, with a nice little spring running, carving a green path downslope, through the brown sagebrush and gray earth. But he rode by what would have been an ideal camp. The first words she'd uttered in three hours had to be those. Ten minutes farther on, with the light definitely gone from the east and not much more than a glow in the west, Slocum called a halt.

"We camp here tonight," he said shortly, swinging his weary legs down from the saddle.

While he was getting his land legs, she said, "Too dark to find wood, Mr. Slocum."

"Be a dry camp, too," he assured her pleasantly.

"May I ask why?" Her face was gritty with dirt.

"Beidler'll look for us beside the water," Slocum said, which was true enough but not much reason to camp a thousand yards from the nearest water when there were plenty of springs all around them and the deep, slow Missouri just a half mile below.

"Come now, Mr. Slocum. Jack Slade used to say that a dry camp is a fool's camp."

"Yeah. But he ain't with us now," Slocum said.

He uncinched the saddle and tossed it down. He'd ground-rein the horses tonight to let them browse the sagebrush tops. Next morning they'd take on water early. He wasn't going to move this camp no matter what

the arrogant woman had to say. From his saddlebags he
got a dirty shirt to rub down his sweaty horse. He started
with the cannon bones and legs, because that is where
horse trouble starts.

Bonnie unsaddled beside him, and watched what he
was doing doubtfully. With a sigh, she turned away from
Slocum and tore a strip off her heavy petticoat. She stood
on tiptoe to reach her horse's back. "Jack used to care for
all the livestock," she said.

"I can tell," Slocum said dryly.

"Sir?"

"Way you're rubbin' that animal, I can see you ain't
had too much practice. Now, do it right, because if you
don't, he'll maybe founder on the morrow, and if he
does, you'll have to walk, because I already killed one
horse carrying double and don't mean to kill another."

She felt like tossing her wet petticoat at his face, but
she swabbed heavily at her horse instead. It was perhaps
nine o'clock. The evening star was up, and the sky was
bright, but the moon was still below the horizon.

He was finished before she was and didn't offer to help
or advise her. She had to do it herself, although she had a
few other things that she wanted to think about.

Slocum lay with his saddle propping him up and a
stick of beef jerky in his hand. He'd spread out his top
saddle blanket, the dry one, to lie on. He had a slicker
unrolled beside the saddle blanket. The slicker lay like a
once-live thing.

Laboriously, she dragged her heavy saddle beside his
and spread her saddle blanket. They smelled of horse
sweat, and she wished for a moment that they'd had time
to pack some simple necessities for the trail. They had
what Slocum carried in his saddlebags, no more or less.

She settled down with a sigh. "Can I have some of
that?" she asked.

Wordlessly he tore off a strand of the beef jerky with

his strong teeth and tossed it to her. When her teeth sliced into the meat, it had some of the qualities of shoe leather; it was that hard. Still, as she gnawed at the tough meat, the juices started down her throat; when they hit her belly, it was like the warmth of new fresh blood, the warmth of life itself. It made her stomach cramp, it was so good. Her teeth tore more strongly, the meat came apart, and for the first time that day a sort of contentment came over her. She wiped her lips and lay back with her head against the smooth saddle.

"Jack—" she began.

"You don't know how sick I am of hearin' about Jack Slade," Slocum said, interrupting. "He wasn't much alive, and he's considerable less now, so I'd take it as a kindness if you'd keep quiet about him."

"I meant to say that Jack Slade would thank you for what you've done," she said icily. Her belly was cold again.

He dug furiously in his saddlebags and pulled out a bottle of whiskey. He took a fast slug and handed it to her. "Here," he said. "Have some of this. I reckon it's what Jack Slade would have done."

In a small voice she said, "I don't drink, thank you."

He said, "Well, I don't either. Least not like Jack Slade used to. Don't you understand, Bonnie? He's hung, and he's got you and me on the run, and hell, he was no damn good for either one of us. You never loved him, did you?"

"What does that have to do with it?"

"Oh, hell. If you don't know, I ain't going to tell you."

Angrily he laid his head back against the saddle and glared at the stars, which twinkled merrily. He wouldn't look at her, but he heard her clothes come off. The top button rustled and then the next. When her dress was off, she tossed it in a heap, and it made quite a different sound

from her petticoat, which followed it. He didn't look.
One thump for one boot, another thump for the second.
His breathing was slower than hers. Without turning his
head, he sat up and unfastened his boots and set them
beside his saddle. Carefully, he put his holstered Colts
one in each boot, with their butts poking out of both
sides of the makeshift pillow, something he'd done
thousands of times before but never, it seemed to him,
with such deliberation, because he could feel her eyes on
him, although he wasn't going to look at her.

She said, "John Slocum, I'd like to thank you."

"For what? You would have been out of that stable
soon as that damn boy's attention was distracted enough
for you to get his pistol. Least that's what you've been
sayin' all day."

"Thanks for sticking by me." There was a tenderness
in her voice, enough so that he could turn and look at
her. He was still angry, but his eyes were drinking her in.
Her breasts were small and high, and her soft belly had
never carried a child. Her arms were smooth and pale,
and her down was darker than her hair.

She felt friendly toward this travel-weary man in his
travel-weary clothes. She thought that John Slocum
would be happier if he didn't take so many things
seriously. He was so touchy about little things, like not
knowing what an ornithologist was. She felt a great
affection for him welling up in her, and she touched his
forehead. He started but didn't pull away.

"I'm sorry, John," she said.

He looked at her eyes then. His own eyes were the
deepest emerald green, and there was an imp somewhere
deep inside those green green eyes that saw all through
her and all through him, too.

Slocum's horse whinnied. John Slocum's hand leaped
to his boots. He had one pistol in his hand and was up on
his haunches in one smooth, slow move. He stayed down

because he didn't want to show, but his gun was in his hand, the hammer was cocked, and he was peering into the gathering darkness of the valley below, waiting for a sign.

Not all the Indians had vanished, and they were still able to rob and sometimes kill if a party seemed weak enough. There were a few road agents despite the vigilantes, and they were merciless.

Slocum waited for a hundred heartbeats before he lay back and waited again, just listening before he took his Colt off cock and slipped it back into his boot.

"Somebody's near," he said. "If it was a band of mustangs, one of them would have answered the whinny."

"It's a new horse to you. Maybe the horse is just skittish."

Stubbornly, Slocum shook his head. "There's something out there. I can feel it."

"Jack Slade used to say that what you can't see shouldn't worry you. He wasn't a worrying sort of man."

Slocum turned over then and grinned at her, fierce as a jack-o'-lantern. "And didn't it serve him? Didn't it bring him up high?"

She stared at him. A tear formed in one eye and cut the grime on her face. Both the horses were grazing now. Slocum cast an ear back downslope but didn't hear a thing.

She said, "I meant to thank you, John. I'm not an educated woman yet, and I don't believe I'm a good woman. But I do know how to keep my promises and pay my debts, and I'd hate to be obliged to you. I would be to you now as a wife is to her husband."

"That sounds more like a disliking kind of thing than a liking kind of thing."

"It's freely given, John. It's freely given."

* * *

Two miles below, on the riverbank, Beamis turned to X. Beidler and said, "Must have been one of them wild mustangs. There's a passel of them up and down the Missouri."

Beidler shrugged. He sat impatiently. He was too short and ungainly to be a good horseman, and he resented any occasion when he had to sit a saddle horse. "That is your concern, Beamis," he said irritably. "You're the tracker. I'm the committeeman. I've never pretended otherwise."

"Well, I don't think it's them," Beamis repeated. "If it was, that horse would have nickered again. It sounded so close, I swore I could have reached out and touched it."

Once more Beidler shrugged. "Then let's continue."

Beamis stood up in his stirrups and scanned the hillside above him, from where the sound had come. "It wasn't Indians," he said hollowly. "Leastways, I don't think it was."

"How far are we from Last Chance Gulch?"

"If it was them, they're doin' what no white man would ever do," Beamis said, thinking out loud, a habit of his. "Campin' up a dry hillside when there's plenty of good water down here. Good fishin', too. Mr. Beidler, when we going to climb down and eat somethin'? My belly's stuck against my backbone."

"How far?"

Beamis groaned. "Three hours in the daylight. Maybe twice that at night. And these horses are wore down to a nubbin, Mr. Beidler. If you press these critters through the night, there's no tellin' how they'll do in the morning."

That wasn't true. Beidler rode a heavy half Morgan, half thoroughbred that wasn't the fastest or most delicate-footed animal that ever walked the face of the earth, but he could carry someone of Beidler's girth all

day and all night for a week if need be. Beamis's horse
was a stubby little grulla mustang as tough as hobnails.

The Vigilance Committee had come up with the horses
and a purse of $50 to help the two warriors. No other
help was forthcoming. The Vigilance Committee's conscience was clean.

It was dark now, but the moon would be up in a half
hour or so, and it would be light enough to see. Beamis
was an unambitious, easygoing man. Generally he introduced himself to strangers as a dirt farmer because he
had ambitions in those directions as soon as his work
with X. Beidler should peter out, and he even owned a
modest spread along the river bottom near Alhambra Hot
Springs. He rode with X. Beidler at Beidler's request.
For the first three years he'd accompanied the vigilante
from mining camp to mining camp. He'd guarded
prisoners, taken prisoners, moved prisoners, and even
tied the rope on a few of them, although his knotting
wasn't quite up to Mr. Beidler's high standards.
Throughout this time, he'd never had occasion to shoot
one of his fellow men or even fire at one. He knew that
he could fire if he had to, but it had never come to that.

For two men who went so heavily armed, they weren't
formidable, although the reputation that preceded them
made strong men blanch. Beidler was no faster with his
special belly guns than Beamis was with his old Army
.44. It was the majesty of the law they represented that
made them formidable. Beamis had come to expect the
average road agent to drop his iron once Beamis came up
on him. Slocum's putting him under the gun last night
had been purely a freak accident.

Beamis remembered the last time he had ridden into
Last Chance Gulch—must have been five years ago
—before he signed on with Mr. X. Beidler. He wished
the moon would come up so that he could see where he
was going. He wished they'd stop for a minute and take

some food. He cut himself a piece of Stoudermire's Plug and stuffed it under his lip, thinking that it would keep his teeth occupied.

Her lips were open under his and cool, neither here nor there, neither resisting nor encouraging. He had agreed, and so she kissed him.

His hands roved her body like other men's hands had roved her body, only perhaps more tentative, not cock-sure. Like the others, the palms of his hands and his fingertips were rough and calloused. She knew about hard hands. Any minute now he'd grab one breast with one hand and push himself into her. That was how it would be.

"I don't hear anybody down there," he said very quietly. He took his hands off her and unbuttoned his flannel shirt. That was a piece of luck. Shirts scratch, and flannel scratched the worst.

His chest was wide and powerful and scarred. Jack Slade's chest had been scarred, too; but Jack's chest had been nearly hairless, and Slocum had wiry black hair running from his paps down to his navel. She looked away, looked up at the stars. She wished that she could burn as brightly as one of those stars and have everybody see it. "What?" He'd said something.

"I asked you if you had any kin still living," he said.

Somewhat angrily, she came back from her contemplation of the stars. "What? What does that have to do with anything?"

"Nothing. I just thought I'd ask. You see that big star up there? I know it's part of the Dipper, but I don't know what it's called. Do you?"

She squinted. "No."

"I thought that with all your readin', you might know something about it. I always wished I knew something about the stars."

"Why are you talking, Mr. Slocum? Shouldn't you be getting on with the job?"

He chuckled. "Plenty of time for that. We got all night ahead of us."

"Well, you may have all night, but I do not. It's been an exhausting day, and if you intend to remain, uh, inert, then I'll want to doze off."

"Well, if you want to, you just go ahead."

She frowned. He must have been pulling his trousers off, because when he faced her, she could feel bare flesh down there, and his knees were bare, too. Well, it would serve him right if right now, right this minute, she closed her eyes. She closed her eyes. She spread her legs to make it easier for him, cocked her knees at the appropriate angle, and prayed that she could go to sleep fast and sleep right through it. And then he began to tickle her in a particularly irritating fashion. Like a feather duster, he brushed her belly and her breasts. The tickle touched her belly and tickled in broad circles up her body until her eyes popped open. It was just the back of his hand.

She meant to say something, but he kissed her, and his kiss was a tickle like his hand had been; quicker than she would have broken it off, he broke it off.

The face that had blotted out the night sky was gone, and he had a hand on her upper thigh now. He was kneading her thigh like soft dough is kneaded, like something live, something tender, something that's good to eat.

His other hand was at her shoulder, just at the nape of her neck, and she hated that hand like she'd hated nothing else in her life. It presumed; up there under her hairline, right where the muscles attach to the skull, he had his hand there, where neither of her husbands had ever touched her. Her muscles knotted and jumped, and she would have prevented it if she had been able. She hissed between her teeth. Her legs closed involuntarily.

Now he had his hands on both her shoulders, kneading them. He wasn't pressing hard, but she was so tight that a gentle touch almost hurt her, and so he almost hurt her, came just this side of frightening her.

She gasped, and his mouth was on hers. She smelled him in her, in her mouth, with his mouth pressed so hard that the bones of their faces met. He pulled away. He kissed her again, quicker this time. He had hold of her hands, and she could not strike him or caress him.

The moon rose like some blind eye over the Big Belt mountains, and his hair was silver, or it was black from moment to moment. Jack Slade had worn his hair long like this. But Jack was dead. It was not Jack beside her now, holding her throat in one hard, calloused hand, feeling the pulse beat at her throat with the palm of his hand. She closed her eyes again because he was kissing her eyelids. He kissed her cheeks. He nuzzled at her neck, and one of her hands was tracing his back, which had less flesh on it than Jack Slade's and was somewhat broader than her first husband's. She liked the touch of his skin under her fingertips, and he must have liked it, too, because he didn't object or push her hand away or get between her legs, which were closed like a day lily after dark.

Deep in her throat she felt something like a chuckle welling up. Hell, she was as strong as he was and every bit as smart, and she could do what she wanted with who she wanted, because she was a free woman and always had been. She dragged him down half across her by sheer force, squeezing him as hard as she could. When she turned him loose, he looked down at her face, washed by the light of the moon. Her hair had gone white in the moonlight, and he brushed a strand of it off her forehead. Her forehead was high and delicate. She was small-boned, this Bonnie.

They kissed. Their breath mingled in their throats, and

THE NECKTIE PARTY   155

they ate of the perfume of each other. Her tongue came out to play and touched against his, first pointed, then flat; then it ducked and ran away, tapping at him from hiding, tapping like a woodpecker taps a tree.

The moon sailed on, white as oyster shells in the moonlight.

He was kissing her at the hollow of her neck, and she was fearful and fluttery as his lips met only a quarter inch over the tube that carried her heart's blood. Her toes were flexing, and she wasn't aware of that, but she was aware of the itch in her toes and at the backs of her knees.

His lips moved down to her breast, and she turned to offer it to him as she would have to an infant. Her toes itched and then the back of her neck as he did something to her breast. His hand was brushing her, stroking her into greater fire, like a cat is stroked, hard and soft. He held her then with that outrageous, insinuating hand, held her hard, and she pushed because she knew that that was how she could get rid of the itch. She rubbed against his hard hand and opened before it. Her hips lifted off the sticky saddle blanket, and the air kissed her bare sweaty back. His mouth was on hers again, and what did he want of her? What did he want?

His eyes were kind, and the laughter in them, the laughter she'd seen earlier, was directed at everything. It was a laughter that finds nothing sacred though many things wonderful.

Her belly was jumping against his face, and his tongue was in her belly button. She wanted to giggle, because this was tickling but not the same way he had tickled her before. She covered her mouth, and the eyes above her fingers were full of laughter and tears.

He put his lips where no man had put lips before, where she'd never thought a man would put his head, so low, down so low. He nibbled at her, and the electric shock shot through her from the back of her heels to the hair on the back of her head.

"Oh, my. Oh, my."

Her belly was settled down, as calm as a lake before a flight of ducks takes off above the still water.

She felt his knees between hers. Somehow, between them, they put him into her.

She sighed as he slid into her, a bit at a time, slid and slid until she knew how much longer she was than she'd ever thought, how much more complex and deep.

She rose to meet him and was glad that she had such power to control her own pleasure. He rested on his hands above her, touching her only with that intimate connection. She climbed him with her fingertips and her heels and hung there like a crab in a basket, plummeting up against him, plummeting into him, surrounding, making him whole.

She found her peace.

8

The fear was in her eyes when he first woke up and caught her looking at him. There was no telling how long she'd been eyeing him that way, as if she had woken up beside some fat, old timber rattler and didn't quite know what to do. As quickly as his eyes found hers, she whipped hers away and looked away, off someplace, as if the most interesting thing in the world was the Missouri River flowing so calmly below them.

"Mornin'," he said, rolling over to reach for his shirt. "Damn, but this ground gets harder every night I lay down on it. You suppose I'm packing it down?"

She didn't so much as chuckle at his joke, which fell over dead and started stinking right away. She got up with the blankets wrapped tightly around her slight shoulders. She watched the river, which was pretty enough, all misty and cool-looking with that metalic sheen under the mist that water gets before the light gains its full strength.

"I was thinkin' of doing a little fishing," Slocum said. "A couple of nice trout would taste awful good right now."

She was looking at the river, but she wasn't thinking about fishing. "I thought we had to get to Last Chance Gulch," she said.

"Oh, hell, another hour or so can't hurt us."

"Weren't you going to see General Meagher?"

He answered stiffly. "I was. I know him from the war. He's a big man in the territory now."

"Well, don't you think we should be saddling up?"

She was probably right. They had to get to Last Chance Gulch and get their story told before Beidler showed up to contradict it. It was important that it happen that way.

John Slocum said, "I have my mouth set for some trout this morning. I hate to do that kind of talking on an empty stomach."

He marched down the side of the hill with his fishing line wrapped around his wrist and a couple of hooks stuck in his shirt pocket. She was to bring the horses down when she was ready.

Slocum marched down the hillside. He wasn't thinking of fish, and his feet were moving in the same determined way they had when he was one of Stonewall Jackson's foot cavalry. His approach startled a couple of mule deer, who bucked up the slope until they saw the horses; then they went on a long, loping diagonal for safety. Slocum saw them jump up, but he didn't pay a bit of attention after that. The hatch was dotting the water with tiny insects, and a couple of ripples showed where big fish had jumped. Routinely, he noted the feeding spots.

His single-barbed hooks were very tiny. He caught a few nice nymphs beside the stream and attached them to the hook before he swung the line over his head, circling it like an old-fashioned slingshot before he let it out to settle lightly on the water.

For a minute, he almost forgot her, watching his line. A big cutthroat trout took his line before it even hit the water, and then, for a few minutes with that tiny hook and light line, he was lost to pure pleasure. The fish fought hard, racing for snags and leaping to hurl the offensive hook out of its mouth, but the hook was well set, and in a few minutes Slocum pulled it onto shore. It was a big, beautiful fish, and Slocum watched the light go out of its eyes, feeling the same regret he always felt when a lovely animal died.

"Where do you want the fire?" There was a whine in her voice.

She had a whole armload of firewood in her hands.

"Come over here. Get a look at this beauty."

She did. She said that it looked like a dead fish. He said that she should build the fire wherever she damn well wanted. Wordlessly, she dumped the sticks on a bare spot, built a pyramid, and scratched it alight. Wordlessly she got a frying pan out of the pack and a piece of leaf lard wrapped in oilskin. She larded the bottom of the pan and said, "Give me."

He handed her the fish. She fried the beautiful thing hot and fast and created two fishes; the burned fish that would come out of the pan and the burned fish that stuck to the bottom of it.

Slocum watched her performance, amazed. In a while he said, "I thought you and me was friends."

"Yeah. Well, don't get any ideas."

"You want some of this fish?"

"I already told you. I want to see General Meagher. I want to get on with my life."

Slocum ate alone, picking the best meat off the bones and leaving the rest on the riverbank for the raccoons. He scrubbed the pan carefully, although she was already mounted and practically twittering with impatience.

When he finally snapped the pack shut and swung aboard, she said, "Jesus."

He said mildly, "Expect I'll be needing that pan sometime again."

The fish lay in his stomach like a stone, and he burped

fishy burps. He felt a little better for eating; once he decided to ignore her, he got so that he could notice things again. A man couldn't spend too much time in country like this locked up in his thoughts or complaints. He spotted Beidler and Beamis's tracks. Fresh tracks stood out from the wagon ruts when there was dew on the ground: two horses, going toward Last Chance Gulch, riding through the night. Slocum was sure that the tracks hadn't been there when they'd camped the previous night, but he didn't make a remark, because he would just as soon strike up a conversation with a spitting catamount. He kept his eye on the country. It could kill him; she could just make him feel bad.

Twice he saw the marks of unshod hooves crossing the trail. One party was dragging a couple of bundles on poles; they were nothing to worry about: a small tribe migrating with its lodges, food stores, and earthly goods. They'd be no danger. The other track was eight unshod ponies, young ones from the looks of their tracks, and he climbed down to examine them, despite Bonnie's ill-concealed impatience. A war party, most likely, going somewhere in a hurry, somewhere to the east. Still, it never paid to try to figure out an Indian. He took his saddle gun and rested it across his pommel until they crossed Beaver Creek, where the trail got wider because Jefferson City was mining a lot of silver and smelting it in Last Chance Gulch, and ore trains had widened the trail and cut the ruts deep into the hard soil.

They passed a buckboard: two old-timers, a man and a woman, on their way into town for provisions. Both men nodded to each other and both women, too. Both men kept one hand on their rifles as they exchanged greetings.

The gulch had been the last chance of the prospectors who had struck paydirt there, the last chance before the ʼbstakes ran out. They'd hit it big. One bar at the foot Gulch yielded $20,000 in clean alluvial gold. Like

THE NECKTIE PARTY 161

Virginia City, nobody found the mother lode, although more than a few had searched upstream for it.

The city spread from the gulch to the hills on either side. It was a smelter town, and in winter months the arsenic fumes from smelting the silver ore got so bad that they had to light their kerosene lanterns at two in the afternoon.

But the smelters changed Last Chance Gulch into something more than a boomtown. Unlike Virginia City, it already had one brick hotel and several brick warehouses. Some of the biggest mining companies in the state kept offices there, although most of them headquartered at Butte City, a hundred miles to the south.

Along with its prosperity, Last Chance Gulch had acquired certain ambitions. It wanted to be the territorial capital, and it looked like it was going to get its wish despite some furious politicking by politicians from Butte City, who wanted that honor themselves.

Jim Hill had promised to bring his railroad right through Last Chance Gulch. When Butte City complained, Hill said that he'd bring it through Butte City, too.

Butte City complained that Last Chance Gulch wasn't much of a name for a territorial capital, which caused some old-timers to bristle and several fistfights but no gunplay. The gulch's partisans didn't argue but set about to change the colorful name to something blander and more political. They thought to name it Helena. But the old-timers threatened to boycott the new name unless the name's partisans could think of something to put some juice back.

General Meagher's presence at Last Chance Gulch, or Helena, was the strongest evidence that this was the new state territorial capital. President Grant had appointed his fellow general Meagher to the position despite Meagher's long service under General Meade, Grant's chief

rival when he commanded the army of the Potomac.
Meagher suited Grant fine, because Meagher was a
politician-general who always made him nervous; where
better to send him than way out west?

Butte City howled when Grant sent Meagher to the
rival capital, and it asked its congressmen to delay
Meagher's appointment, which they did. Consequently,
he was in the peculiar position of a nominee without
confirmation. Since Congress had adjourned shortly after
refusing to consider his appointment, Meagher was a
man with and without a job.

He was immensely popular throughout the state,
although he was no particular friend of the vigilantes.
Slocum had counted on that to get Bonnie Slade a fair
trial instead of a necktie party. That was his plan, but she
didn't want to stand any sort of trial, fair or not.

"You want to hit the hoot owl trail?" he asked.

"I don't care. I don't care at all." There was a stubborn
curve to her lip. "I never did anything wrong. I don't
want to stand any trial."

"If MacArdle had any kin, they wouldn't agree with
you."

"What's that to me? You can stand trial if you want to,
but I certainly don't want to stand up in front of a bunch
of strangers and pretend a remorse I do not feel.
MacArdle caused Jack Slade to die as sure as if he'd put
a gun to his head. I gave him a fair chance to fight me,
and when he wouldn't, I shot him dead. What else could
I have done?"

Slocum saw it much the same way, but he didn't feel
like saying so, because he had to turn this willful filly's
head before she dashed herself to pieces.

"If you don't get a fair trial, you'll get an unfair one.
Beidler will hunt you so long as you stay in the West."

The two of them rode into Last Chance Gulch. There
were high boardwalks on one side of the road, low ones

on the other. When it rained, the whole street got greasy with slippery, yellow mud. When it was dry, the same mud cracked and pulverized into dust and lay on any piece of wood or projection large enough to provide a shelf for it.

The ore wagons stirred up the dust, the horsemen wore it, the pedestrians swallowed it, and it hung on the few evergreens in the fancy backyards. Otherwise the hills around town were quite bare. Smelters burn a lot of wood, and every day the wagons rolled into the smelters with ricks of wood for the insatiable fires. The smelter melted ore day and night, and residents found plenty to complain about in the smoke and the stink, but nobody complained about the money. Last Chance Gulch had the Woodsmen of the World, the Odd Fellows, and the Masons. It had Lutheran, Baptist, and Presbyterian churches already, and the Catholics had started talk about a diocese. Boosters were happy, and the chamber of commerce had already decided on a site for the capitol once Congress got around to it. They'd hold the election right here in Montana Territory, but the votes would be counted in Last Chance Gulch.

The old-timers began to say that it would be okay if they renamed the town so long as they mispronounced Helena as "Hell-ina" to show some spirit. The boosters said that even with that pronunciation, the name was a damn sight better than Last Chance Gulch.

It was a home for optimists and boomers. Already some of the women had formed a temperance league and sent petitions to get some of the saloon busters to town. The saloon busters replied that they'd wait a few years, because their experience in the far West was that men beat them up or women beat them up before they really got started breaking up the joints.

Last Chance Gulch wasn't quite tamed but was well on its way.

The dust settled on Slocum's face, and the town was noisy. He rode near, or he wouldn't have heard a word she was saying, not that he cared. She had been talking foolishness.

"I don't want a trial," she said. "If Mr. Beidler wants me to leave the West, why, so I shall. I shall go east. That's where I can best pursue my education."

"You talk fancy for someone who's read a dozen books," Slocum remarked.

That got her. She turned hot eyes on him. "Shame, sir! Shame!"

It had gotten to be too much. Slocum stopped his horse in the middle of the street and sawed at his reins. The hurt animal pranced over to a hitch rail, where Slocum dismounted quickly and looped his lines over the rail. He never looked back to see whether she was following. He didn't care.

The sign hanging over the boardwalk proclaimed this to be the "Capital Saloon," which might have been premature but didn't hurt business.

Damn fool woman, hog stubborn and ignorant. She'd have her own way if she had to hang for it. Well, so be it. It was no concern of his!

Slocum forgot torching the livery, forgot shooting the judge's son. In his anger, he had no ties with Bonnie Slade more permanent than the sperm he'd put into her all night long, which was, no doubt, leaking out of her now.

The Capital Saloon was cool and quiet and a relief from all the noise from the street, which ceased as soon as he closed the door behind him.

It was a new kind of saloon. Planks across the whiskey barrels were still the standard model in small camps across the territory. Two walls were spanned by a dark mahogany bar with high pilasters and arches over the bottles and glassware. The tables were covered with green baize and were large enough to accommodate a six-handed poker game. A few men in the back were playing blackjack but not very seriously. Slocum wondered whether the place got livelier at night. He was feeling lucky.

He didn't think about the woman he'd abandoned so suddenly, didn't think about her at all.

It was nearly ten by the big, old Waterbury clock on the back wall. A couple of tables were pulled together against one wall with a dozen men, all deferring to a man Slocum recognized. He hadn't meant to find General Meagher this quickly.

Meagher was a big man, a little more gray than Slocum remembered. His smile was quite as ready, and his leonine manner hadn't changed a bit. Slocum had met the general just once, before Gettysburg, when he'd bodyguarded General Lee for a parley with the Yanks. Slocum was a lieutenant of sharpshooters then and unused to the honor of accompanying Massa Robert, a man the entire Army adored. He was very conscious of his responsibilities and not unconvinced that the Yanks meant to murder his charge. His uniform was borrowed from a member of Lee's own staff, but his repeating Spencer carbine was his own. He didn't leave it with his horse but carried it right into the parley. Meade was there, along with Meagher and the aides. Lee and Slocum represented the Confederacy.

Meade and Meagher seemed inclined to call the whole thing off. Meagher wanted to fight. (Slocum didn't think he'd ever forget his big Irish face, red and choleric and hollering that "This damned rebellion can be stopped here. At this spot.") Lee, who was invariably polite, had smiled calmly, and Slocum tightened up on his Spencer. He was not to talk, but nobody had said anything about glaring, which he did until Meagher commented that if "General Lee's soldiers were all so fierce as the young lieutenant, then the Union cause was in terrible danger." He said that before he laughed. Slocum didn't forget that laugh, either. The next day it was Meagher's New Yorkers and the Pennsylvanians under Butler who broke the greatest Confederate charge of the war on Cemetery Ridge at Gettysburg.

The war had taken them to different places then, which was fairly lucky for General Meagher, because Slocum was one of the two or three finest shots among a group of crack shots. Singled out to be a sharpshooter and issued an officer's spyglass and an extra-long-barreled Schuetze rifle, he killed many men that day but never the man his glass was searching for.

That was years ago. It had been a long ride, and he was conscious of how filthy he was and how much he wanted a drink. He ordered a glass of Centennial beer and sat down facing the general's party. The beer was cool and fresh and had a creamy head. He drained his mug in four quick swallows and set the mug back on the waiter's tray before the man could get away.

"Another," he said.

"That'll be four bits." The waiter hadn't seen this travel-stained pilgrim before and wasn't going to chase him through the dusty streets if he skipped out on his tab.

Slocum looked at him for a long minute, and the waiter got a little itchy under the collar. He said, "Right away, sir."

Slocum paid with dust, pinching it onto the baize of the tablecloth.

"Yes, sir," the waiter said for no particular reason.

Slocum watched the men coming and going at Meagher's table. Before each stranger could speak, somebody at the table vouched for him. Then General Meagher flashed his big smile and half rose to take the man's hand. The man sat in the chair at the general's right long enough to tell a joke or two and offer a toast (which most of those at the table acknowledged by lifting their own glasses but not drinking), and then he'd bend his head at the general's ear. Sometimes Meagher received the news thoughtfully, sometimes he was surprised; once he was angry and squeezed the messenger's arm until the man protested. Nobody sat in the chair for long. Sometimes Meagher spoke a few words to the men at the table or the messenger; sometimes he just nodded, and the man left.

John Slocum's heart was going pretty fast, because he was more used to trying his luck with gunplay than politics. Still, even though Bonnie Slade was a terrible pain in the ass, he owed her enough to speak his piece. He lifted his second mug, drained it, stood up, and started for Meagher's table just as a waiter banged through the back room with Meagher's lunch.

The waiter had a big silver tray balanced high, a towel over his right arm, and a big smile on his face just like a beer poster.

Meagher's compadres must have been waiting for the meal, because one or two of them applauded when they saw it coming. A couple of them cleared away room in the center of Meagher's table for the tray. The lower table would have to wait its turn.

John Slocum stood beside the empty chair and asked, "Mind if I sit in?"

Meagher had eyes for the food. The man on the other side of the chair got up, looked at Slocum, and said politely that this was General Meagher's table, and it was a private party; anybody can make a mistake, it's natural. The big man didn't sit down, and the way he held his hands and the slightly punched-up look of his face told Slocum most of what he needed to know.

"The general and me met at Gettysburg," Slocum said.

The pugilist spoke softly again. "If you're here to put the arm on the general or ask him for a loan, I do all that sort of business for the general."

"Name's John Slocum. I come over to speak to Meagher, and I guess I'll do it."

The general had a drumstick in his hand, but he looked around to quell what promised to get rough in a second. "Sit down. Sit down, Slocum. Two minutes. State your proposition, sir."

"I was with Lee at Gettysburg. You was arguin' that we fight. Meade didn't want to fight us, but you wouldn't let us pass."

Meagher's eyes were big and blue and round as plates. They shrank slightly, and Slocum felt like a map being read. Finally, Meagher snapped his fingers together.

"Now. Now I remember! You were so much younger then. And you had the meanest eyes I ever saw on another human being. You've changed some."

"Expect so." John Slocum leaned back in his chair. He could have done with a bite to eat but didn't know how to go about getting it.

Meagher munched on his drumstick. "Meade was such a waffler. He flapped in every breeze like the flag at the flagpole. We weren't situated quite right for General Meade," he said ironically, with the air of a man who's won his throw of the dice.

"You was situated well enough," Slocum said. If there was a bitter edge in his voice, who could blame him?

"My doing." Meagher took a big bite of his drumstick. He wiped his mouth on a linen napkin. He took a sip of beer. He took another bite from the drumstick. "What do you want?" He chewed the words with the drumstick.

It wasn't going to be any good. Any fool could see that, and John Slocum was no fool. Still, all a man can do is try. "The damn vigilantes are hunting an innocent," Slocum said.

The general went on eating. He leaned over to an aide and said, "Get over to Senator Mueller's home. Tell him he must go along on the choice of the capital or we'll open some competition for that feed monopoly of his."

The aide nodded and hurried off. Other diners came into the saloon, although it was early for lunch.

"I have nothing to do with the vigilantes," Meagher said. "They do not operate in Helena." It was funny hearing him say the name he wanted like it was an accomplished fact. "I believe they have acted in some of our smaller communities to rid their towns of riffraff."

"She's a woman."

"A woman?" General Meagher knew the value of calculated disinterest.

"Bonnie Slade. She's not yet thirty. She shot a man in Virginia City. She gave him every chance to go for her iron. He'd caused her husband's death."

The general produced a big, bland smile. "Sounds sticky to me, Slocum. Here, let me order you a beer."

The friendliness, Slocum guessed, was because he hoped to hear something useful. The Virginia City contingent was inclined to vote for Butte City as the state capital. There could be no harm in listening. He inclined his ear, like he did for every other petitioner, and John Slocum told him the whole story. Slocum told of a rowdy but not dangerous drunk who was strung up by the Vigilance Committee in a fit of pique.

"Who did you say spoke up against it?"

"Judge Batesworth. Batesworth and all his friends."

"Just what did the judge say and where?"

Slocum told him. Meagher nodded thoughtfully. Judge Batesworth would be a good man to have aboard.

"But it was X. Beidler who promoted the hanging of this unfortunate woman's husband?"

"It was."

General Meagher wasn't one of X. Beidler's greatest fans; but Beidler had some powerful backers, men whom it was unwise to cross. Privately, Meagher thought that

Beidler was a murderous little ferret. Publicly, he praised him for getting down there in the pit with the animals and doing the kind of necessary, thankless work few men would care to do. The "necessary" was, of course, a concession.

Slocum told how he had set Bonnie Slade free even while Judge Batesworth had been arguing for her release with Beidler.

"You stole your horses?"

Slocum didn't fall into that trap. Nothing could save a horse thief. "No, sir! I bought my horses from O. K. Harris that very night and took a bill of sale to prove it. I didn't want Beidler talking against us."

Meagher nodded. He was beginning to reevaluate John Slocum. He asked him what he'd done so long ago, the day they fought at Gettysburg.

"I was a sharpshooter." Slocum grinned. "I kind of specialized in generals and line officers."

"Did you now?" A big smile. "Clarence, have you heard this? This man hunted me once, but it was my charmed day."

Many a man might have been horrified by meeting his unsuccessful murderer, but Meagher was delighted. It was a proof of his strength and of his luck, and so he bought John Slocum another beer. The waiters were gathered at the front of the saloon, and he had to send his bodyguard after the beer because he couldn't get their attention.

Meagher asked, "Did you kill anybody getting the woman away from that kangaroo court?"

"Nope. Shot one fellow in the leg muscle. He'll walk with a limp, but he'll walk again."

Meagher finally looked at Slocum with those disingenuous dinner-plate eyes. "And what exactly do you wish of me?" he asked.

"No more than the law allows."

There was a distant rumbling like an ore tipple dropping ore. The waiters were watching something outside in the street.

"I am very fond of the law myself," Meagher said.

"I've had great good fortune lately," John Slocum said. "Won nearly five pounds of gold from a man named Murphy in an honest game of poker. I was thinkin' about making a little political contribution."

"First you try to kill me, then you try to buy me." Meagher's voice was flat and thoughtful.

Slocum didn't know what to say, and so he said nothing.

Meagher's smile was like the sun coming out. He said that it was good for a man to know who his friends were, and six pounds of gold was a fine amount for a campaign contribution.

"Five pounds," Slocum said. "I only won five pounds. I wasn't trying to bargain with you, General. I was trying to get Bonnie Slade a fair trial."

"A trial?" Meagher let slip his surprise. He was thinking that the man was here to buy a pardon, not a trial. A trial he could have had for three pounds of gold, but a pardon would have been six. Five pounds was too much or too little, and it disconcerted him. Still, every man needs money. He sent an aide outside with instructions to bring Slocum's saddlebag from the big roan gelding at the rail. "And if you so much as put your hand inside, MacCarthy, I'll cut if off at the wrist. You do understand?"

In just a moment John Slocum's saddlebags were on the floor at Meagher's side. "You get it. I have no great urge to paw through your dirty underthings."

"General." MacCarthy was speaking.

"Just a minute. I want to see if this man knows how to weigh gold."

Slocum tossed his poke on the table.

"General, there's two hundred men out in the street, and they are lookin' to string somebody up!"

The poke sat in the center of the table, heavy with its contents. Meagher's hand drew back without touching it. "What was that again?"

MacCarthy repeated it. He added the intelligence that the mob meant to hang a woman. Lynch mobs were common enough, but women were infrequent victims, and some of Meagher's pals got up and started toward the front door of the Capital Saloon. They let pass a stocky German-looking fellow all dressed in black.

"Excuse me," he said.

"Out of the way, Mac," they said, craning their necks and nudging when the waiters wouldn't abandon the choicest views.

"Good afternoon, Mr. Slocum," X. Beidler said. He didn't ask to sit. He stood among the empty chairs and faced the three seated men: Meagher, his bodyguard, and Slocum. "General. I am pleased to see you well. How goes your plan to rename this town?"

"Just fine, Beidler. What are you doing this far north?"

Beidler took off his hat, dabbed at his sweaty pate with his handkerchief, and replaced his hat. He adjusted his hat. He sighed. "Business, General. Always business."

"I hear you had a little trouble over at Virginia City the other day," Meagher said.

Beidler's face lit up with false surprise. "Oh, where did you hear that?"

Meagher nodded at Slocum. "I hear you hanged a man who hadn't done a thing!"

"You heard that? Mr. Slocum, have you been spreading rumors? How should I say it? Slocum, have you been filling the general's ears with bullshit?"

Slocum's smile was easy and unconcerned. He had one hand in his lap, and his Colt Navy was in his hand. "You callin' me a liar?" he asked.

"I suppose I must be." Beidler cocked his head to consider the matter. "Yes, I am. Definitely."

"Now, exactly who did this Slade kill?" Meagher asked.

Beidler grinned. "An ounce of prevention, General, is worth a pound of cure."

"So he hadn't actually killed anyone?"

"Not yet. No." Beidler wasn't uncomfortable. His certainty was making John Slocum uncomfortable.

"I see. An ounce of prevention is a novel theory of jurisprudence."

Beidler shrugged. "It's a new country, General. Sometimes we don't have time to observe the niceties."

"I see."

Beidler reached over and pushed at the gold poke. "A wager, General? Mr. Slocum is making you a wager? I know that John Slocum is a wagering man, and I have heard that you are, too."

A chant started up outside. "Beidler. We want Beidler. Hurry up in there."

One of Meagher's aides came back long enough to bend and whisper something. "Temper of the crowd" was all Slocum heard.

"If I were you, General, I would not take Mr. Slocum's wager. I am not one to advise a man what he should do with his life, but I am here to arrest John Slocum for jailbreak and for arson and for shooting Judge Batesworth's son."

"Batesworth? You son of a bitch, you didn't tell me it was Batesworth's son." The general shoved Slocum's bribe back at him. The general stood up and snatched his black hat from the wall hanger, and then he called for his aides. "I believe we have business down the street," he said. "MacCarthy, why don't you go and see if the back door is open?" He didn't say good-bye to X. Beidler or to

John Slocum, either. Although most of his aides wanted to stay and watch the fun, they followed him.

Beidler shook his head. "He is a fine, law-abiding man," he said. "And a general, too. In my family I was always brought up to respect the military man, the man like Frederick the Great. I wonder if Frederick ever took a bribe." The smile he directed at John Slocum was a hangman's smile, a smile of perfect complicity, a smile of perfect friendship and understanding. "Come now, John. We have Mrs. Slade outdoors, and you must stand up beside her and be judged. Give me your guns."

"How'd you like a new navel?"

Beidler had been so certain. He had tracked down a hundred scoundrels and faced them with the might of Right behind him. Some scoundrels tried to talk him out of it. Some tried to appeal to a love of family and friends. Some waxed eloquent, promising reform. One or two mentioned secrets they held over important men. Some offered gold. One man offered his wife, a comely woman of twenty summers, and his own lifetime services as manservant and slave.

Beidler had hanged them all.

Now John Slocum got up, so easily and gracefully that you'd have to look twice to notice the Colt revolver he held on Beidler's middle.

"Come now," Beidler said. "Don't be melodramatic. This isn't Uncle Tom's cabin, you know." He reached toward Slocum. He meant to accept the gun. Slocum drew back the hammer.

A drop of sweat started at X. Beidler's hairline, wobbled down his nose, and hung there. His hand stayed in place, and his eyes worked to read the other man's intentions. He read only his own death. "You'll never get through the crowd."

"Well, that should be a great satisfaction to you," Slocum said. "If we die at the same time, will we get buried at the same time? I cut you down, they cut me down. A couple of days for everybody to look the bodies over and pay their respects, and we get planted. Sure, they'd plant us the same day. I expect you'd be a bigger draw because of all this vigilante business. I expect there'd be men come to your funeral from all over the state. Ranchers, big mine owners. Hell, Meagher'll be there with bells on. They'll all be wearin' the solemnest expressions." Slocum laughed. "Seems a shame to have to miss out on that."

"And you?"

"Oh, I expect I won't be nearly the draw you will, but. . . ."

"But?"

"I'll be just as dead. You ready?"

X. Beidler watched his own hand as it retracted toward him. He felt like he was going to lose control of his bowels, and he actually had to bear down for a moment to keep the unspeakable from happening.

The green in Slocum's eyes was like a cat's gleam, a cruel cat but graceful. "I understand you wear belly guns," he said noncommittally.

Wordlessly, Beidler handed Slocum his specially modified Colts, and Slocum made them vanish under his shirt. The whole exchange went unnoticed by the waiters and bartenders, who were pressed against the front windows, watching where a crowd had a woman up on a fifty-gallon barrel right across the street, right in front of the General Merchandise with its farm implements and barrels of flour. They had her on the round top of a barrel somebody had rolled onto the boardwalk, and they had a rope around her neck. Her pale face was blank with shock.

"Beidler! Beidler! Get it over with!"

John Slocum put the belly guns and his poke in the saddlebags. He holstered his Colt. He slung the saddlebags over his shoulder and said, "Lead the way, friend. It's you they're callin' for."

All morning Beamis and Beidler had been scouring the town, searching out vigilantes. Beamis worked the low bars, and Beidler tried to see the important men in town. Beamis had the easier task. Beidler's friends sensed something they'd just as soon keep upwind of. The crowd caught Bonnie Slade just three minutes after John Slocum had drawn up in front of the saloon and set her adrift. Two men stepped off the sidewalk, took hold of her horse's reins, and said, "Are you Mrs. Slade?" And Beamis had said that he was mighty sorry about it, but sometimes things happened this way.

There were miners and homesteaders and sweepers and unemployed teamsters. They were out for a show. Probably they couldn't have come up with $2,000 among the two hundred of them, and only a few dozen weapons. Many were drunk, and more were acting like they were so that they wouldn't be responsible for hanging a woman. She'd done murder. They knew that. And she sure as hell hadn't denied it when Beidler's man fired the question at her: "Do you, Bonnie Slade, admit to having killed Jacob MacArdle?" She'd said yes. They'd heard it with their own ears.

When the front door of the Capital Saloon swung open, the crowd cheered. It was X. Beidler and a stranger, side by side, just as chummy as could be. Many had the idea that Beidler had gone inside the saloon to make an arrest. Maybe he'd make an arrest later.

"Let's hang her," somebody said.

The cry went up. It mounted, paused, and then died out because everybody wanted to hear what Beidler was going to say. If he said yes, then they could hang her without nightmares.

Good thing she was in shock and wouldn't feel a thing. The crowd was thickest in the center as Beidler and the tall stranger pressed forward. Beidler's man, Beamis, was on the far side behind the woman and didn't see who was walking with Beidler, although he heard the cheer.

Slocum's face seemed inappropriate to the occasion. He was grinning like there was nothing in the world that could give him more pleasure than the grisly event. Even those who were really thrilled by the prospect of seeing a woman hang—and there were a few of those—thought that his expression was indecent.

John Slocum was having a hell of a time. The next few minutes would probably end his life on earth, but he figured that he was lucky it should end while he was in his prime of strength and full of piss and vinegar. Nobody could hope for anything better than to die while he was feeling good.

Beidler walked at his elbow, docile as a sheep to the slaughter. The crowd parted before them, their cheers dying.

Slocum vaulted onto the hitch rack beside the barrel. He reached down with one Colt and tapped Beidler on the top of the head. He made no attempt to hide his motion, but it was so swift and Beidler dropped out of sight so quickly that nobody thought that he saw what he had seen, and nobody moved an inch. John Slocum unslung his pack saddle and clamped it between his knees. He looked at Bonnie Slade, whose eyes were stunned. Her breathing was rapid. He could see her chest move.

He spoke conversationally right into her ear. "Bonnie," he said, "if you don't wake up in the next couple minutes, you're going to be back with old Jack Slade again."

9

She blinked and then blinked again. John Slocum didn't have much extra time, but he meant for her to have every second. He stood with his saddlebags between his clenched knees, perched on an eight-inch hitch rail, watching the crowd for intention to form, in their manner, their posture, and their guns. It was a bad crowd: early-morning drunks, men whose hands had gone soft from weeks without work, men who fed on fantasies and the fantastical.

She turned her head. Her tongue moistened her lips. Her eyes were big-pupiled and out of focus. Already she was halfway gone, halfway a resident of shadowland.

"Hey! Who the hell are you?"

"Where's Beidler?"

Words would destroy him yet. There was a shuffle on the boardwalk as Beamis pressed through the crowd. Slocum was of no moment. Beamis's first responsibility was, always, to the man who filled his dinner pail. He was using muscle now to get through the mob, which was thick at the foot of the gallows.

"Just who the hell you think you are?"

The recognition came into Bonnie Slade's eyes, an arrival from an arduous journey across mountains and plains. "John?"

"Uh-huh." He spoke through his teeth as convicts speak, because it wouldn't take much to make this crowd jump up and fasten the rope around his own foolish neck. He dug inside the saddlebags and undid the poke.

These men were gold miners. When a total stranger got up on a hitch rail and hurled a handful of gold nuggets over their heads, it didn't take long.

"By God, boys. It's paydirt!"

"Whoopee!"

Slocum raked the nuggets caught in his clawed hand and hurled them far out over the crowd in a great sweeping gesture.

The crowd went down like mowed wheat. Like heathens bowing to some strange god, they got down head to head, scratching for the gold.

"I got me a good one. God, what a beaut!"

An admirer took time to punch the discoverer, and the two men rolled around in the crowd, knocking other men over and causing more strife wherever they rolled.

There were three hundred men in that crowd, but not one man's eye was on John Slocum. Slocum lifted the rope off Bonnie Slade's head. She knew who he was and was looking at him with eyes that held equal measures of hope and fear.

"It'll be all right." He took time to say that.

"By God, that's John Slocum, and he's killed X. Beidler!" Beamis was at his boss's side, mistaking the patch of blood on top of his head for a fatal wound. Beamis fumbled for his holster flap.

Slocum winced. "Oh, God damn it. Don't do that, you fool."

Beamis's fingers scrabbled the flap open and tugged on the butt of the pistol. He was down on one knee beside Beidler's supine form, looking up at John Slocum, which constituted a pretty awkward position. Slocum had taken one of Beidler's belly guns out of the saddlebag. He wasn't sighting it, he was just nestling it in his right hand, with something very much like pity in his eyes.

Beamis had his gun out, and he lifted it, swiftly as he could. The gun lifted of its own volition, avenging the humiliation, the discomforts, the difficulties of his life.

Slocum leaned down and smacked him hard with his boss's belly gun. He dropped.

That opened the festivities. Most of the men behind the gallows had squeezed into the street for the golden shower. Some of them kept on looking. They'd seen fights before, but not nuggets in the street. These men were too drunk to find anything and examined each scrap of horse droppings like it might be something rare and precious. One drunk hauled his hogleg out of his pocket and, hoping to blow Slocum off the hitch rail, took the back off the skull of a man who was in the crowd hoping to prevent the lynching. The drunk sat down from the recoil, and Slocum's snapped shot at him went over his head and did no particular damage.

Slocum stepped off the gallows platform with one arm around Bonnie's waist and the other around the birds-head butt of a belly gun. The hammer hung under his thumb, and if he fell, he was going to take at least one man with him. He hurried down the street. A big man stepped out with a carbine held tightly in his hands, and then Slocum snapped off four shots and dropped the belly gun on the boardwalk. The bullets took the man in the hip and spun him into the street, screaming. He wasn't dying, but he screamed like he was. That scream stopped the gold hunt in downtown Last Chance Gulch. That scream sent men scattering as the gunplay hadn't. Bodies went every which way.

Shots were more frequent, although aim wasn't anything to brag about. Slocum helped Bonnie Slade onto her horse. The woman was dead weight or next to it, and he hoped that she had enough strength to ride.

The other belly gun was nestled in the palm of his hand, because it was so small, it wouldn't seem too threatening. It wouldn't, he hoped, call any more attention to himself than he already enjoyed.

Root hog or die, he thought, and he was smiling as he got up on his big roan horse. The next few minutes would tell him all he needed to know about the horse's speed. A bullet snapped past his head. One man, a clerk, from the looks of him, had taken refuge behind a watering trough across the street and was shooting at John Slocum, with more courage than skill, with what looked to be a short-barreled banker's Colt.

Slocum let three bullets chase one another out of the belly gun, pointing in his general direction to disturb the man's aim, which it did. One bullet entered his right eye and broke his skull, following the crease of bone around the outside of his head. It should have killed him, but instead it made him one-eyed and ugly.

"Go, woman," Slocum muttered. The belly gun spoke twice more and followed its mate into the dust.

A rifle was banging away, and it was a good thing the shooter had no skill, because he couldn't have had better targets: two horsemen moving slow, at a range just longer than point blank. John Slocum put a few bullets into the sill of the window the rifleman was shooting from, and the man ducked inside for cover. It felt good to have his own pistols in his hand. Beidler's belly guns just didn't have the accuracy. With his own Colts he could kill a man at a hundred yards, on foot or on horseback. Beidler's guns hadn't been good for a quarter that distance.

Bonnie Slade had her horse trotting now, and they weren't too far from the corner where the gulch took a swerve, and the street with it. Slocum reached over and swatted her pony with his hat, and the animal moved right into a gait somewhere between a lope and a gallop. She was leaning back in the saddle instead of forward, and he was afraid that she was going to fall off. He put the reins between his teeth, the way he'd done years ago when he rode with Quantrill, and he screamed that high warbling rebel yell.

Men who were about to fire hesitated because of that scream, just long enough for him to be fifty feet farther down the street. His own Colt was talking, too. He used his lead to keep heads down or drive men indoors. He had all the easy targets any man wanted, but if he ever did get free of this mess, it was better to leave as many alive as possible. One shot smacked a rifle butt right out of a man's hand. It was a lucky bullet, but he had meant it.

His horse was stretched out full gallop, and he lay so far forward along the horse's neck that it would have been easier to kill the horse than him. By the time those with any sense decided to do that, the animal's tail was going around the corner of the brick warehouse that hid the next stretch of Alder Gulch from their view.

Slocum booted his big roan horse, and the two fugitives pelted down the gulch.

It was noon, and men were outside the gates of the lumberyards and the liveries, eating lunch. There was a crash of gunfire from up the hill. Just as men started moving up the hill to find out what was happening, a couple of horses came ripping down the gulch like the devil himself was behind. The gulch wasn't an easy passage. There were horsemen, buckboards, and a few ore wagons drawn over while the driver had a quick beer at his favorite saloon, leaving not enough room to pass.

Men said that it was like a circus, the way the two of them came, the woman loose as a clown on her big black animal. The animal knew what he was up to and let her ride without demanding much help. He ducked the ore wagons and buckboards and forced single horsemen onto the sidewalk when he thundered by. She flopped all over the saddle. Sometimes she hung on with both hands and sometimes with one hand, while the other hand clutched at her saddle horn. She swayed back and forth in the saddle, lively as a badly secured bag of feed.

Behind the clown was the equestrian. His roan threatened to pass the big black but always drew back at the last moment. The roan's rider was live, as much a part of the riding as the horse, snugged down and helping the animal swerve with his body, muscling through spaces scarcely wide enough to allow them passage. Once he jumped the tongue of an ore wagon that had stopped across the street; the black made it past the lead horses, and the roan jumped the tongue between the horses and their driver. He had the traces wrapped around his wrist, and when the hurtling animal hit them with its chest, the unfortunate teamster was dragged out of his seat and dumped like he'd been plucked out by an invisible hand.

It was a fine October day with the pale sky overhead and just a touch of the breeze that had frosted the high pastures the previous night. The air was dry, and sound carried a long way. Some men later claimed to have heard Slocum's rebel yell from the shantytown at the bottom of the gulch, nearly a half mile from where the necktie party had gathered.

A wagon: around it. A horseman: pass him by. Two horsemen: split them. A buckboard: push onto the boardwalk. A pedestrian: ass over teakettle.

The gulch flattened out with surprising speed, flattened onto high plains and shacks. They galloped past the washlines and the loafers sitting on packing crates in the front yard.

Women called out to one another to watch them go by "Like hellions," as Mrs. Murphy put it so aptly.

One road connected the camps of Alder Gulch, Silver City, Bird's Eye, Gloster, and Great Falls. The trail they had followed from Virginia City passed into the Big Belts at the Gates of the Mountains and became something other than it had been. That country was left for Crows, Blackfeet, Flathead, and occasional Sioux. There was no gold found east of Confederate Gulch and no prospectors, either. The heavily traveled road north was corduroyed at the muddy spots. Hardly anyone took the trail.

John Slocum's instincts were for speed and cunning. When the two were at odds, he always went for cunning. He did so now, abandoning the clear road north for the indistinct path that veered toward the Gates of the Mountains. He tugged at Bonnie's bridle.

She gave him an angry glance. There was more intelligence in that glance than in anything else she'd done so far.

When Last Chance Gulch was just a mote over their shoulders, Slocum slowed his horse and, again by taking the bridle, hers.

The trail dipped into a shallow wash and up the other side. The going was steep, and Slocum dismounted and took both animals by the lines to help them up the far side. When they'd scrambled up the talus slope, he walked beside their heads, saying all the soothing, comforting things he knew how to say. She was screwed around in her saddle with both eyes on the back trail, squinting from the bright sun.

Slocum's knees were going to start to tremble in a moment, and so he stopped. He leaned against his horse's heaving brisket and said, "Whoooe. Whooee. I believe we stung them some that time. My God, they're going to be mad. My God!"

She looked at him, uncomprehending. His laughter was a maniac's symptom, and his belly was rumbling from a hysterical remark. She was still coming back. Her body felt strange to her, as if she were a new tenant in it. He laughed long and alone, until he'd laughed himself sane again and the trembling was gone from his legs. He remounted and nudged his horse up beside hers.

"You feelin' right?" he asked.

"Yes."

"Well, that's good, now. Now I'm going to tell you here what I mean to do, because I might fall by the wayside or get shot or something, and I want to tell you the plan I figured out. That's right, you just keep that horse at a walk. We got a couple hundred miles to go before we find safety, and I don't want these animals failing us."

"Plan?" She sounded like she was still stupefied.

"Yes, ma'am. Couple little ideas I had how we can get out of this damn big territory before X. Beidler turns us into long-necked giraffes."

"Giraffes?"

"Never mind. See how the river cuts into that canyon there? Well, we'll be following it, because it's slow and we're not likely to run into anyone else unless we run into a redskin. We'll be traveling slow and traveling long. Beidler will go after us on the main road for sure. Now listen."

Hours later, X. Beidler waited outside the little roadhouse that was the only sign of human habitation at Prickly Pear, Montana Territory, and bit his lip to contain his curses. The Helena–Great Falls road ran wide and smooth, a hundred fifty miles north to Great Falls, twenty miles south to Last Chance Gulch. "Helena," he said.

"Huh?"

Beamis was sitting with a bottle of beer propped up against his saddle horn, which he'd purchased from the same roadhouse keeper who'd assured Beidler that no pair of riders had come by this morning, no man and no woman, no couple like Beidler described.

"They should leave the name what it was," Beidler said. "Last Chance Gulch was good enough for them when they were taking her wealth. Now they want to rename her Helena."

"You want some of this beer, boss? You talk like a man who's been hit on the head."

Beidler was brought back to consciousness only a few minutes after Slocum and Bonnie made good their escape. Beamis had sluiced a bucket of water over his face. Beidler's hair and shirt had dried flaky with blood, and his right eye was kind of squinched up because his head hurt like hell and squinching helped the pain a little.

Meagher would do nothing for him, absolutely nothing. X. Beidler cooled his heels a precious two hours trying to persuade Meagher to form a posse and run the bastards down.

Meagher weighed the pros and cons. When X. Beidler was delayed enough to give the fugitives a lead, he smiled and said that he had no jurisdiction because he wasn't sworn in yet. If the lynch mob wanted to follow Beidler, they were certainly welcome to, but nobody had got killed. If a few feeling were hurt, so be it.

"You see this as a chance to embarrass me," Beidler said.

Meagher smiled and said, "Come to think of it, it won't do me any harm."

Meagher returned Beidler's belly guns.

Beidler tried to gather a posse on his own hook, but the same men who'd been so willing to hang Bonnie Slade were less willing to follow her and an armed companion on a long chase. Slocum's lead was now three hours. Most of the members of the necktie party had arrived on foot because they couldn't afford a horse, others owned no firearms, and others wanted to lie around in the long cool afternoon. Beamis was for that, having had the scare of his life that morning, not to mention a headache, but Beidler was implacable. They rode out, just the two of them, making no attempt to track Slocum in the hard surface of the road. At the bottom of the gulch, they asked which way the riders had turned, and Mrs. Murphy told them about hellions turning north.

North was Great Falls and Fort Benton and most of the warrior tribes. Maybe Slocum meant to hide the girl in the rough country. Maybe he had kin in Great Falls. X. Beidler wished that he knew him better. He knew him as a gambler and a gunman and a fugitive but wished he had a better understanding of him as a man. It would be so much easier to hang him as a man.

They questioned other travelers on the wide road north. They passed the point where the trail to the river crossed, and paid no attention to it. Beamis saw horse marks but didn't know whose they were. Beidler had taken a fierce shot from the pistol barrel and sat in his saddle like a sick, old man. He had nothing left but his will.

"Boss, maybe we should find us some shade and lie down. We been hard treated, boss."

Beidler answered between hurt teeth: "I hope advising me does not become a regular habit."

Beamis shut up then, and the two men plodded north. They didn't have the stomach for a gallop, and Beamis stopped to ask all the questions, with Beidler sitting on his horse and rocking back and forth. Many of the travelers Beamis spoke to were spooked about that crazy-looking, sick-looking man dressed in a bloody black suit. Beamis usually made up some quick story about road agents to explain his boss's peculiar appearance.

"I ain't seen nobody like you describe, son."

Nobody had. Fifteen miles up the road it was obvious that the fugitives hadn't passed this way, but Beidler said to press on, and so they did.

Beamis was sipping at his beer and listening to his grumbling stomach. He said, "Well, boss, I don't believe that man lied to us. They ain't come past Prickly Pear, that's sure."

"But they are going north?"

Beamis shrugged. "So that lady said at the foot of Alder Gulch."

"We go north. They should never name it Helena."

Beamis took his time finishing his beer but finally pointed his horse north. The boss was the boss, even if he did have a crack in his skull.

The fugitives node north, north by east, north by west, wherever the trail turned. Slocum walked the horses or walked beside them, alternating every couple of hours. When Bonnie Slade had come partway out of shock, he told her to get down and walk, too. She didn't give him any argument, and although she was weak, she didn't ask for any special favors.

All day they traveled. A good tracker might have followed them, and they'd made no attempt to conceal their trail.

Although they didn't stop, except once to let the horses water, the feeling was growing in John Slocum that maybe there wouldn't be much of a posse after them. He didn't know why he felt that way and didn't count on the feeling, but it made him feel pretty good. Every time the trail climbed up high enough to overlook their back trail, he eyed the land very carefully. Twice he took out the collapsible spyglass from his saddlebags and saw nothing then, either.

He started humming a campaign song called "Stonewall Jackson's Way." He was still alive, wasn't he? Alive and lucky. He shouldn't have walked out of that one, should have been kicking at the air instead of riding out across the wild country with a beautiful woman at his side. She was silent, thinking that Slocum was too private a man to interrupt his thoughts. They crossed Indian sign beside a shallow place in the river where good horses could ford. It looked like a big war party heading east, the same direction the other party had been heading. No skin off his nose. They weren't any threat on the wrong side of the Missouri. They passed Rock Creek and crossed Dog Creek. Some of the time they rode, and some of the time they walked. Slocum still kept an eye on his back trail, but he wasn't worried.

It started getting gaudy at sunset, with purple and red and velvet streams cascading in the west. He found the sort of place he was thinking about, a narrow deer meadow beside the stream where the horses could graze. He asked her to gather some dead grass out of the deer beds for tinder, and he broke some branches off a snag at the river's edge for fuel. He built his fire in the circle of stones other travelers had used, perhaps for hundreds of years.

The mosquitoes weren't so bad this late in the season. They had laid out their gear and got a fire going before the last of the sunset cast its message across the sky. Then they boiled some tomatoes out of the can. Slocum fried the last of his salt pork and dropped it in a can of beans, which then joined the tomatoes in the big skillet. The coffee pot started burbling, and he put it on a rock to keep hot. He poured a shot of rye into his metal cup, added coffee, and handed it to the woman, who sat on the blanket beside him. She took it without a word. She held it between the palms of her hands, warming them. There was a chill in the air, a reminder of the winter ahead.

She was looking at the sunset. She said, "I suppose you want me to thank you."

It kind of disappointed him, to hear that coming from her when she'd been thoughtful all afternoon.

"No," she amended herself, "I didn't mean what I said. I meant to thank you, but it came out wrong." She looked him square in the face. "You know how it is."

"Sure."

She took a sip of the aromatic coffee, and the heat went to her skin right away, warming the blood in her tissues.

She spoke to him and to herself and to whatever god was listening. She said, "I don't think many are snatched back once they've gone over to the other side, and I had gone over, John. Do you know how I hate you sometimes, how easily I can hate you? Do you know how much better it was for me in a world I can control? There aren't any real worlds, John, or false ones, either, just plenty of worlds. And in some worlds you have control, and in others you don't. I live up to my bargains."

"I'd say so, yes." He was remembering particularly how she'd been when they slept together last night, but MacArdle had been gunned down because of her obligations, too. He said, "In this world, sometimes it's better to lie and cheat a little."

She laughed. "You're a fine one to talk."

He grinned, knowing himself for the stern fool he often was. "Sure," he said.

"I kept all my obligations to Jack Slade and some I didn't really have, but I didn't give him anything important, so I cheated him. Do you see that?"

"That damn dinner smells good."

"Damn it, listen to me!"

"I will. I will. Reach me that plate. I only got one, just like there's only one cup." He spoke pointedly, and she passed the cup. It warmed him no less certainly than it had warmed her.

He handed her the plate first, although his stomach was growling, because those were the manners he'd learned at his mama's knee.

Bonnie wanted to talk. She said, "If I didn't love him, I shouldn't have married him. Do you see that?"

John Slocum's stomach was reminding him that sometimes manners were a too-much thing. He said, "Eat."

She said, "If you want to eat, go ahead. I can take care of myself."

"I can see that." But he took the plate and started quelling his body riot.

She hiccoughed. He put down the spoon after a couple of good scoops. She hiccoughed again.

"What the hell's the matter now?"

She opened her mouth and howled. She howled with laughter like a coyote howls, like a wolf howls, like every creature who can know joy howls. She howled until her body was howling, and she rolled on the ground, laughing as the life flowed through her again. The tears ran out of her eyes so hot and fast that she was flooded. Some got into her nose, and she sneezed and laughed again. He was laughing, too, with her, with his head back, laughing because it felt so good to be out there beside their fire, alone in the wilderness and alive.

She wound down through a few more sneezes and some hiccoughs. She swallowed her hiccoughs with hot coffee, and it eased the place where her waist hurt from laughing. Slocum scraped his spoon against the metal plate with every bite he took, and if she hadn't been sick of laughing, that tiny scrape would have set her off again.

"Pass me the grub," she said. "Partner."

It was pretty good. The fire was small. The grass of the deer meadow stretched around them higher than their campsite, and the horses munched and walked around with the sound of rustling silk.

The next day was cooler and a little overcast, one of those days when every sagebrush seems brilliantly distinct, when even the massed formations of sandstone buttes are sharp as knives. They traveled as they had the day before, watchfully and silently. Before leaving Virginia City, Slocum had loaded up on oats, but they had used up the last of them that morning, which was how he always remembered that morning: the morning he finished the oats. He caught a pair of nice Dolly Varden trout that afternoon and wrapped them in wet grass to keep them cool. Once again they rode late before they camped. They camped a hundred yards up Stickney Creek, just above the flats where it joins the bigger river. Tall Douglas firs and beds of sweet needles at night. When Bonnie Slade fried the trout, she did them fine, didn't burn them at all. Slocum knew better than to compliment her for not burning the fish.

The next morning he met the horses' expectancy with empty hands and the excuse that this trip wasn't his idea, either. They didn't buy it, but they didn't get any grain.

Slocum rode into the yard of St. Peter's Mission about noon and was able to buy some grain for the horses. The missionaries offered the weary travelers a fine lunch of bread, white cheese, and potato soup. They didn't ask any questions. Slocum left a thumb-sized gold nugget in the poor box. This woman made Slocum feel good, he decided.

They circled the bluffs that lay above the trading town of Great Falls. A few miles above the river falls that Lewis and Clark had portaged in three arduous days, the town was small but prospering. Some of the small cattle outfits had started to headquarter there, and the railroad would arrive next season. On the other side of the mountains, Alder Gulch couldn't hope to see its first train for eighteen months. Slocum avoided the town of Great Falls. The closest they ever got to it was on the top of the Missouri River bluffs. Great Falls was a vigilante town, much like any other town in the territory. It was like Billings. It was a cow town, and cowboys dearly love to string up thieves before their Saturday night drunk. They had hanged more here than in most other towns in the territory.

Beidler would have arrived before them. Slocum was beginning to feel that he knew X. Beidler, knew the way his mind worked. He would have hated to meet X. Beidler on the ground of his choice after he'd been humiliated, the unforgiving little kraut.

They stayed on the western side of the river and camped a couple of miles past Box Elder Creek in a draw just under the tip of the high bluffs. It was five hundred feet to the water below, which glistened like a sword. A couple of vultures were riding the thermals over the water, high and silent. Tonight they'd make a meal of the single loaf of bread the missionaries had let them have. It wasn't much, but washed down with a canteen of tin-tasting water, it filled them up.

She stood in the sunlight-sunset and took off her travel-weary clothes. He thought that she looked very young. He loved the curve of her spine, and each bump in it was dear to him. They made wet and slow love, locked in each other's limbs, penetrating each other's bodies until the red sun went down and the only light was in their eyes.

Fort Benton, Montana Territory, was the end point of the steamboat runs from St. Louis. Fort Benton was an important town, the terminus for all the river shipping as well as Army headquarters for operations against the remaining Indian populations.

A hundred and eighty steamboats and sidewheelers came upriver in 1864. Five years later, the number had doubled, and the docks spread upstream and downstream from the fort itself for two miles on both sides of the river. The town was on the west side, and a ferry carried passengers from the other side. Nails and gunpowder, millstones and flannel, clockworks, Colts, and King James Bibles: whatever the frontier needed, and it needed tons of goods every year. Pilgrims come west to find their fortune or drown their sorrows, to find adventure or escape the consequences of adventure.

The boats were shallow-draft. As dangerous as the river was below St. Louis, above it was ten times worse, and it took an experienced pilot and a cautious captain to bring those boats across bars where the difference between deep and shallow water was inches.

Fort Benton was quite a town. During the spring and summer, when the military was active and as many as five boats arrived daily, it was a rowdy town, too.

They rode down River Street toward the Palmer House, which was the fanciest hotel in town and the one Slocum felt that he deserved. His poke was still part full, with plenty of money. After one fire, one near-lynching, and a couple of shooting scrapes, he felt that he deserved something fine and a bath.

The clerk at the desk was a little snotty because, as anyone could judge from the well-dressed men sitting on the Palmer House's front porch, the hotel was particular about its clientele.

It was not so particular once Slocum pinched out a little gold. It was good to be rich. He could get used to it.

They took one room. The bathhouse behind the hotel was divided for male and female guests, but as Bonnie lay luxuriating in the hot water, she could hear him singing on the other side of the partition.

They had a change of clothes brought in from the dry-goods store. She looked at the bed and said, "I haven't slept in a bed for so long."

He was fastening a string tie. Today he was dressed like a high roller, in a gray pinstripe three-piece suit with frock coat, string tie, and ruffled shirt. He was smoking a good cigar.

He said that she could stay there and sleep. She opened the window and took in a deep breath.

"I'll be going down. I mean to get out of here on an early steamer. Tomorrow if I can."

That had been his plan.

The boats made a few stops en route to St. Louis, where Slocum figured that he might be more welcome than he was in Montana Territory. There was Judith, just the other side of the badlands. Judith was just near the Bear Paw Mountains, and maybe he'd spend the winter locked up in some high mountain vastness, trapping. There was something appealing about the idea, something calm. Or he could get off at Fort Buford, where the Yellowstone ran into the Missouri, and see whether he could find out what all this Indian trouble was about.

One thing was sure: A sidewheeler could slip downstream faster than any number of vigilantes on horseback.

The officious desk clerk was considerably thawed by Slocum's new clothes and by the fact that he paid for everything with gold.

"No, sir," the clerk said. "There's only the *Rosebud* in town. All the other captains have gone. There's talk of ice on the river upstream, and nobody wants to be here for winter lockup."

"For God's sake, it's just the fall."

"It's October, mid-October."

"Oh."

"Captain Cooper is the *Rosebud*'s skipper. You can find him in the saloon bar: tall fellow, skinny as a rake. Hair like yours, black and longish. He'll be passing the time at cards. Captain Cooper stays with us every time he comes up the river. He'll be hauling hides back down-stream and is waiting for the last of them to come in."

"How long?"

"Three or four days, a week at most. He won't be able to wait much longer than that." The clerk nodded at his own judgment.

John Slocum felt his heart sink. Hell, if there'd been a boat out of there this afternoon, they would have been on it. No room was too nice when a man had a posse on his heels.

Maybe the clerk had it wrong. Slocum went outside. The Palmer House faced one side of Fort Benton's parade ground. The east side of the parade ground was the waterfront. There were sidewheelers at the docks tied up for the season, and many of them had already been hauled up onto the shore, where the winter ice couldn't damage them.

The rail of the *Rosebud* was just three feet above the water, and the front quarter of it was piled with bales of hides. There were thousands of bales, about the size of bales of cotton: buffalo hides for the coatmakers and shoemakers and saddlemakers back east. There were more bales waiting on the wharf. A couple of men were loading the hides with prybars, gangplanks, and wheel-barrows. Slocum wished that they would hurry. They surely weren't moving as fast as they could.

He was thoughtful returning to the hotel. He wondered whether they should ride to the next point downriver. They could wait at the wood station for the steamboat. Nobody would be looking for them at a wood station, and Beidler would get around to looking in Fort Benton if he hadn't already.

The clerk at the Palmer House looked at him a little peculiarly, but he'd done that before. Slocum shifted his holsters.

The saloon was a single big room on the river side of

the Palmer House. It was a favorite with the Army officers and bankers and steamship brokers of Fort Benton, and the high rollers gathered there, too. The place was half full with twenty souls, and the talk was low and quiet. The men wore the badges of their standing and occupations, military hats or cattlemen's somber Stetsons. Several examined Slocum, but nobody expressed any particular interest. A man beside the window had to be the captain of the *Rosebud*. He was playing a quiet game of solitaire while two other men at his table talked to each other.

Slocum leaned up against the bar and ordered a whiskey and ditch. The whiskey was good; the ditch water tasted like ditch water.

X. Beidler spotted him and came over to his elbow. "Good afternoon, John Slocum," he said in a conversational tone of voice.

"You again."

"I am a persistent man, Mr. Slocum."

"Can't say I'm pleased to see you, but I'll buy you a drink for that little love tap I gave you back in Last Chance Gulch. Barkeep!"

Beidler took his drink and drank it. He wore a patch on his forehead just below the temple. He was quite neat again, quite the dude.

"I should probably warn you that Mr. Beamis hopes to join us here tomorrow with a party from Great Falls. I thank you for the drink."

Slocum felt a little sick, but he took and drank his drink, stood up straight, and did his best not to show it. "Sometimes, Mr. Beidler, I've thought of cutting you down."

Beidler opened his coat. He had no belly guns. He let it flap shut and rebuttoned it.

"I've given up guns, you see. I'm quite unarmed except for righteousness."

Slocum sighed. "Unarmed. Beidler, you disappoint me. You don't know how bad."

10

Slocum felt little of the intimacy Beidler had tried to create the last time they met, the executioner's intimacy. He was annoyed and weary. "I've seen men hit softer who didn't get around good for a month."

Somewhat primly, Beidler admitted that he sometimes saw double. He added that momentary weakness shouldn't deter a man.

"Momentary?" Slocum asked. He tossed off his drink without waiting for an answer that Beidler didn't give, anyway. "Where's your iron?" he asked. "Those two ugly guns you were carrying. I suspect somebody got them back to you."

"Yes. They were returned to me. Thank you for showing me the error of my ways."

"Which error was that?" Slocum's face was lemon sour.

"I am no gunman, sir. My authority does not come from my ability with firearms. There are men who are skilled in their use who—"

"Shit."

"I am a man of the law, Mr. Slocum," Beidler said with considerable dignity.

"You're a man who likes to see other men at the end of a rope."

Beidler thought for a moment before he said, "Yes. That, too."

Beidler offered to buy the next round, but Slocum said that he wouldn't want to take anything from Beidler's hands that Beidler would give willingly. He also said something about Beidler being the poorest man he'd ever met. He didn't want another drink. Beidler's presence had chased the ease right out of him. "Suppose I go to the fort commander," he said.

Beidler smiled. "He is a soldier. This is a civilian matter. Go to him if you wish."

"Me and Bonnie can just ride out of here."

"Of course you can. You can ride to the east or west, north or south, and I will follow."

"I could murder you."

Beidler's smile was small, shaped like a cupid's smile, and mean clear through. "I don't believe you're that sort of man." Beidler inclined his head in a mock bow and left.

Slocum watched Beidler's back and then looked at his empty whiskey glass. His foot was up on the bar rail, and he was pressed comfortably into the bar. He wondered where he'd gone wrong. He didn't want so much, after all. He wanted to see some new country, have a few friends, live his own life. Why did this little son of a bitch have such a strong desire to put a length of hemp around his neck? He shook his head. The bartender took that for a signal and brought him another shot and ditch that he didn't want. Well, if he stopped feeling sorry for himself and thought about his problem, he could come up with a solution. He hadn't seen too many jobs needing to be done that he couldn't do. That's all this was: just another job.

It would take Beamis less time to round up his vigilantes than Beidler had said. If Beamis left as soon as he and Beidler spotted their quarry, it would take eight hours each way on the trail and maybe an hour and a half to gather a bunch of volunteer hangmen. Slocum counted the hours and decided that Beamis could get there easily by tomorrow morning at dawn. After a night of hard riding, the vigilantes wouldn't be too eager to listen to John Slocum explain how he was an upstanding citizen and Mrs. Slade was another pillar of the community.

He could ride away, but Beidler would follow. He and Beamis would follow anywhere they could put together a mob. John Slocum could do more riding than he'd already done, but he didn't know how much more of it the woman could stand. Already some of the fat had started to melt off her arms and around her ribs, and she hadn't been a hefty woman to start with.

It made a man feel itchy to think about the possibilities. It made him want to hunt Beidler down or buy a couple of new horses with some of his remaining gold and just gallop the hell away and ignore the consequences.

But that was weariness and panic speaking.

Slocum took a drink of river water, ignoring the shot glass that sat on the bar beside it. He left a pinch of gold dust on the highly polished bar and put his back against the bar to survey the room.

The men in that room were the powerful men of Fort Benton, Montana Territory, and none of them were weak as willows. They were the boss wolves of this particular pack, and most of them went armed.

Except for a few men so deep in conversation that they couldn't be jarred, and the captain of the *Rosebud* shuffling his deck of cards, these men felt the weight of John Slocum's gaze and lifted their eyes to find the green-eyed stranger staring at them, asking for information. The gaze was sharp and sure, and no two men took it the same way. The banker thought that it was the gaze of a bank robber sizing him up. One military officer thought that it was a scout's gaze, eyes that scoured the depths of a hundred miles of plains, looking for Indian sign. One young man dropped his eyes away because he thought that Slocum's gaze was a terrible imposition.

Every man thought that the glance was for him alone, and most of the men it touched could remember the lone figure with the green eyes and black hair years later: a stranger in a neat gray pinstripe suit, no gold watch chain, and high black riding boots instead of shoes. Two ebony pistol butts protruded from his coat, and he was smiling.

Captain Cooper looked up as John Slocum pulled out a chair. Slocum had the knack of willing himself into an attitude; when he sat down at Cooper's table, he was what he seemed: a prosperous traveler accustomed to the better things. From the rough look of his hands, he'd done some hard work in his day, but so had most mine owners and most ranch owners.

He had a military carriage and a slight swagger that meant Confederate, not Yank. When he spoke, Slocum's voice carried more of a drawl than usual. "Afternoon, sir. I see you take pleasure with the pasteboards."

Captain Cooper dealt himself a hand of solitaire. He played automatically while he tried to place the face. He'd never seen the man before. "We've had fine weather for this time of the year," he said.

"It's snowing in the Belts," Slocum informed him.

The captain cocked his head. His hands put a ten on a red jack. "You're traveling from the south, then?"

The question was nicely phrased, because Slocum didn't have to answer it. In country where it's sometimes impolite to ask a man for his origins or destination, the question could have been handled a thousand ways. "Yes," Slocum said. "Bound for St. Louis."

The captain perked up his ears. He had a full load of

deck cargo contracted for this trip, but the *Rosebud* carried a dozen passengers this late in the season, and it was only half full. This man looked like someone who could easily pay passage, and those broad shoulders might be useful if they had to walk the shallow craft off some sandbar or hack her out of the ice. Captain Cooper stuck out his hand and introduced himself. He added the information that two of the best staterooms on the *Rosebud* were unoccupied, "the best passenger cabins on the river." For some reason the captain winked at this, which was somewhat startling.

Slocum nodded his head. "Me and my wife. . . ." he began.

"You'll be wanting the stern cabin, then. That's the biggest we have on the *Rosebud*. None of my crew have space like that, and my own cabin isn't one whit larger. We hope to make a quick trip to St. Louis, and though we can't hope to exceed our flying trip in August, when we did the journey in twelve days, we will make good speed."

"Twelve days?"

"Yes, sir. We were light-laden for the journey. On a wager."

Slocum seemed interested, and the captain was not immune to flattery.

"Captain Rexrode of the *Judith* wagered me $500 that his vessel could beat me, wharfside to wharfside. Rexrode is a proud man, you understand, and the *Judith* is powered by an Ingersoll and Harris two-stroke engine with a boiler of a thousand gallons, wood or coal. And the *Judith* has a reputation as a fast boat."

"I'll buy a drink, if I might."

The captain had earned his smile in a gallant race three months ago. Of course, Slocum could buy him a drink. The captain talked of a race in high slack water, a race in which the *Judith* got hung up three times and the

Rosebud had her bow punctured by a snag where there'd never been a snag before. "Two hours from impact to floating again," he bragged.

"Two hours. My."

The captain described his river knowledge and his daring, shooting rapids rather than taking the safe route through slack water. "Almost," he said. "Almost I could try to best my record."

"And why not?"

"You can't make time in this water. Not with a full load of buffalo hides."

Slocum affected surprise.

"Oh, yes. The *Rosebud* will be loaded stem to stern with heaps of stinking buffalo hides." The captain looked gloomy. "Can't make any speed with that load."

"Twelve days," Slocum said dreamily. "It's quite a feat and quite a triumph."

Again Captain Cooper winked at him. Again the wink was disconcerting. "And I found ways to spend the $500," he said.

Slocum laughed. "I'll bet." Then, although he wasn't even slightly hungry, because he sensed that the captain was, he asked about the food at the hotel. The captain relaxed slightly and said that it was pretty good, and perhaps they could dine together, being as they were obviously congenial gentlemen. Slocum said sure, why not, and stuck out his hand. "My handle's Slocum, John Slocum. Me and my wife have traveled from Virginia City."

"You look like a lawyer to me, sir."

"I do have some slight acquaintance with the law, but I'm in mining. I've a nice property up in the Bitterroots, near the headwaters of Pilgrim Creek. You don't know it, of course, but Pilgrim Creek feeds direct into Alder Gulch."

The captain snapped his fingers, "Ah. That I have

heard of. It is where they pan gold in sluices in the middle of town.".

"Yes, from Virginia City. Well, my little property is a good ways about it, where the canyon walls come in pretty close. Looks to be a bigger river traveled that country once, but it's dried up to not more than a trickle now."

Slocum didn't know how much he would have to tell this riverboat captain before the man got the point. He wanted the man to understand that this passenger might very well own a claim that sat squarely on top of the Virginia City mother lode. The captain didn't know anything about mining and geology, and so Slocum brought him up to date while they ate a good meal of elk steaks and potatoes, canned beans and tomatoes.

Finally the captain got the point. "Then you must be sitting on a fabulous treasure."

Slocum smiled man to man. He said, "No way of telling about those things, of course. Except for me and the Indians, nobody has prospected up that far, and I have left a small company of well-armed fellows behind to deter claim jumpers. We intend to start our shaft in the spring, and I mean to seek mining machinery in St. Louis. All that machinery will have to go upriver on steamboats, of course. Would you recommend we buy our own sidewheeler?"

Captain Cooper nearly choked on his apple pie. He spit out a piece of it, which he hoped Slocum didn't notice. He coughed into his linen handkerchief, and his face got little bursts of color in each high cheekbone. The captain looked like he had a little Indian blood in him somewhere.

"I wouldn't advise that, John," the captain said rather solemnly. "Riverboating is a real art. You have to know the river. You have to know the freighting business. You have to know your men. And if you make a mistake, you can wipe out your entire investment in the blink of an eye. It's a chancy trade to master just as you're sinking all your attention into the earth." He chuckled at his own pun, and Slocum chuckled, too, although he thought that it wasn't much.

The food had been good. A black waiter went around lighting the kerosene lanterns along the walls. The river went by outside their window, and the two men turned to face it.

"It's some piece of water," Slocum said admiringly.

"Two thousand miles from here to St. Louis and another two to New Orleans and the Gulf."

"You could take this *Rosebud* all the way to New Orleans?"

The captain took the question at face value and spoke at length about what the trip would mean to a shallow-draft boat. While he spoke knowingly of sandbars and riffles, snags and famous steamboats, Slocum's mind drifted along. He thought about far-off places he'd never seen before. When he thought about those places, he always imagined himself alone and never put a woman in the picture. He had never been to New Orleans; the closest he'd ever come was Kansas during the war. Never been to Natchez, either. He had crossed the river into Vicksburg when Grant had it under siege many years ago.

"And then the Quarter itself."

"Huh?"

Again that wink. "The French Quarter. The Old Quarter, sir. Surely you've heard of it?"

Slocum recovered. "Indeed I have." He had a twitch in his right eye, but he was damned if he would let it turn into a wink. He said, "I know how it is with you bachelors."

Two could play at the stuffy game, and Slocum

enjoyed discomfiting the captain. He spoke about the pleasures of the bachelor life, of saloons and whorehouses. He mentioned Storeyville, the greatest whorehouse in New Orleans, but added that unfortunately he couldn't visit it because of the little lady. That's what he called Bonnie Slade: "the little lady."

"I, too, have a better half," the captain confessed. He ordered brandy and said that the river would freeze over in a week or so. He could feel it in his bones. The *Rosebud* would be slicing through a skin of ice before the trip was finished.

Slocum noted how happily the man fled back into talk of his beloved river. Captain Cooper was one of those men who have to keep their attention riveted on something all the time lest they see what they don't wish to. He asked, "Wouldn't it be wise to depart sooner?"

The captain bemoaned his contract with the hide dealers. He hadn't expected to be carrying so much of a low-paying cargo. The whole cargo would net him only a few hundred dollars. "The fare for the finest stateroom on the river is $30 to St. Louis," he annonced grandly.

Slocum waved a hand. "Done," he said.

The captain sipped at his brandy, lit a cigar, and announced that life was fine for a man who knew how to take advantage of it. The waiter came over and said that after eight o'clock the tables were reserved for those who wanted to play cards.

"I'm comfortable," Slocum said, slipping him a cartwheel. A few men were waiting for their spot. Slocum nodded to them but didn't shift his eyes. "I don't suppose. . . ." he asked.

Captain Cooper fancied himself a poker player and won more often than he lost. He opened his hands in the gesture of a man who accepts any suggestion.

"Fine, then." Slocum lit a cigar and invited the other men to make up a game. One was a surveyor for the

Army. The other, a much younger man, was Fort
Benton's new painless dentist.

The game was the usual: stud or draw, five card, no
sandbagging with a check and raise, table stakes. The
surveyor and dentist chatted with the riverboat captain
while Slocum went to the hotel safe for his poke. He met
Bonnie in the lobby. Bonnie looked good enough to eat.
She hugged him.

"Where does a girl get a bite to eat in this joint?" she
asked.

Slocum told her about the dining room. He told her
that she was Mrs. John Slocum of Virginia City.

"Isn't that going a little too fast?"

"We're quite the respectable couple," he explained.
"I've got a claim on Pilgrim Creek. We're a company.
Going to St. Louis for mining machinery."

"Whoa. Slow down. Hold your horses, partner."

"Beidler's here."

Her hand went up to her cheek. She aged.

"Nothing to get worried about. He's by himself. No
mob."

"He . . . he. . . ."

"Yeah. He means us no good. But he can't hurt us so
long as we play it right."

She looked a little faint, and he told her to get some
red meat into her as quickly as she could. After she ate
something, she should come over to the poker table,
where she was to be charming to Captain Cooper. "Hair
like mine, gangly pale-faced fellow. Hair's pretty long."

"John, I never have charmed a man in my life."

"Well, you had better learn. We ain't out of the noose
yet."

She said that she'd do her best, and he returned to the
table alone. He dropped the poke on the table. The others
looked at it. Gold country was a hundred miles away,

and in Fort Benton most men dealt with coin and greenbacks.

Slocum said, "I'm going to ask to trade gold for cash before we begin."

The hotel had to bring its scale to weigh the handfuls Slocum pulled from his sack. Plenty hadn't seen a heap of gold like that before, and the curious came around to the table while the hotel clerk balanced the delicate scales. Slocum's poke was back inside his jacket. He'd managed to make it seem like there were plenty more handfuls where that one had come from.

"It's quite a thing," the dentist said, "to see that much precious metal all at once."

"Outside the mouth," his companion joked.

That brought a laugh. But Slocum couldn't joke, because every man knows that there isn't anything so serious as one's own money. Captain Cooper asked whether he could pick up one of the nuggets, and Slocum said, "Sure, go ahead." He didn't say that there was more where that came from, but that was what he hoped to convey.

The hotel bought $1,800 in gold. The clerk had to go to the safe. Slocum insisted on gold coins, and everybody nodded because that was the savvy thing to do. The clerk was annoyed at the extra work involved but brightened when Slocum put a double eagle in his hand.

Nobody missed the exchange; nobody was meant to. When the gold coins were stacked in front of him, U.S. gold in tens and twenties and California gold in octagonal fifties, it was as if a wall separated him from the other players. Everybody looked at it. You could hear men breathing hard. It looked like a lot of money laid out that way.

Slocum smiled, shrugged, put all but $100 into the poke, and dropped the poke carelessly at his foot. "Hell," he said. "I suppose that was bad manners. Where

I come from, we're always at the weighin' and countin' of gold. I meant to play a friendly game. I ain't no high-stakes card player."

But Captain Cooper was. When Slocum dropped his poke casually under the table, the captain's heart dropped with it.

In a rather strangled voice, he asked, "Another brandy, sir?"

"Sure. Why not?" Slocum tossed in a dollar for ante.

The game went faster than the dentist and his pal had intended, at least at first, when a dollar ante looked big to them. Slocum started losing immediately, betting a pair against three of a kind, underbetting his winning hands. Before the deal had gone around the table twice, the ante was up to $5, and Slocum was pushing his third stack of gold into the pot. He smiled wanly.

"You boys are just too damn good for me," he said.

The painless dentist hadn't seen so much cash at one time in his life, and the cards were running with him. His chuckle was brief as he dealt a round of stud.

Slocum ordered round after round of brandy for the table. The captain bought a few rounds and the surveyor one, but the dentist was too busy making money to think about mundane matters. He swallowed his booze as quickly as it came. Every time the waiter came, Slocum returned his old glass for a fresh one, and each time the old glass was half full. The dining room was closing. Twice men came over and asked to sit in, but both times the dentist said that he liked a four-handed game. The gold coins built up in front of him, a modest replica of Slocum's wall.

Slocum watched Bonnie eating. When she was done she left, and it was a half hour before she came downstairs again. She wore her dressy gown, bought that afternoon, and her blond hair was brushed into a luster and tied by a single ribbon so that it flowed behind her, loose and free as a girl's tresses.

Slocum folded a good hand and rose when she came to the table. "Gentlemen, I'd like you to meet the woman who did me the honor five years ago, and never a moment I haven't honored her since."

Bonnie handled the simpering speech pretty well. She deferred to her husband's words, managed to come up with a demure smile, and said how she was delighted, and wasn't Fort Benton wonderful. She mentioned the wonderful river.

"Two thousand miles of it to St. Louis," the captain said.

The dentist said that they should play poker.

"Oh, hell." Slocum laughed. "You been cleaning me all night, and I do aim to get even. You just rest a bit while my wife gets a chance to say hello."

The smile he turned on her was affable and bland. She flashed him one quick dagger before her face assumed an expression no less false than his own. "I hope you're not betting the Homestake," she said. "Our mine," she explained.

"It certainly sounds like a promising venture," the captain said.

"Well." She laughed. "My husband thinks so, but you men are always so optimistic."

Dutifully, everybody laughed. The dentist tapped his cards on the table. His partner shot him a look, and the dentist tried to keep his impatience under tighter rein.

Bonnie held the captain's hand a little longer than she had to when she was introduced, the way she'd seen fancy ladies do in Denver.

In Denver, John Slocum and Bonnie couldn't have passed, but they were deep inside the territories, and Bonnie's flaws were interpreted by her audience as motes in their own vision.

Slocum patted the back of her hand. "Do stand behind me, dear," he said. "You bring me luck."

When they sat down again, she put both hands on his shoulders and gave him a quick squeeze before she asked, "Have you seen anything of that little German fellow? That lunatic?"

Slocum picked up her cue. "Why, yes, dear. I saw him in the lobby this afternoon."

Again she squeezed. "Do any of you gentlemen know a man who calls himself X. Beidler?"

When they shook their heads, her voice achieved the gaiety it had only desired before. " 'X.,' honestly. I wonder what that stands for? Extra? Xavier? X marks the spot?" Her laughter trilled.

Slocum didn't know where she wanted to go, but he was willing to tag along. "He's quite harmless," he suggested.

"Harmless? The man's out of his mind. He goes about stopping people on the street. Says he's some sort of hangman. He wants to hang them. You may think that harmless, but I find it grisly and not suitable talk for a lady's ears."

"Don't worry, dear," Slocum said, but he was thinking: Nice, nice.

The dentist won the interrupted hand with two jacks. With Slocum folded, there was hardly enough in it to count. Just $50, which was a good month's pay for a young dentist. How easily we get accustomed to wealth.

Slocum played slowly for a bit, folding frequently and betting small. He told stories while he played, stories of the early days in Virginia City. He made it sound like he'd been part of Bill Fairweather's original party. "Of course, I wasn't quite growed." He laughed. "I tended the horses and washed the pots on that little journey. Bu it gave me my first taste for huntin' gold. One thing about it"—he leaned over confidentially—"gold comes easy." He laughed at the unfinished joke. "But it goes out easier than it comes."

The dentist meant to say, "Don't you know how to bet anymore?" but bit his tongue. He'd counted and recounted the money in front of him, nearly $400. His partner had $100 in gold showing, and the captain was $300 ahead for the evening. The play went on as before, with Slocum trickling out the dollars and buying most of the drinks.

Bonnie watched it all. Although she didn't know how to play, she could see the flow of gold as easily as anyone. Slocum's shoulders under her hands were easy and loose.

It got toward midnight when X. Beidler walked back into the room. He'd been looking for Bonnie, and his eyes lit up. He came right over to the table. He said, "I'm glad to see you two enjoying yourselves." He was quite ready to enjoy a bit of cat and mouse.

Bonnie Slade drew back in complete, unfeigned revulsion. "Won't anyone protect me from this man?"

Slocum remained seated. He figured the dentist to rise to the occasion. He had the most at stake. The captain got up, too, probably thinking about mining machinery.

Beidler didn't know the reason for the angry looks, but he knew them for what they were and chose a wrong tack immediately. "This woman," he said, "is a murderer. This man burned down a livery."

Slocum folded his hand reluctantly, got to his feet, and faced Beidler. He said, "Yes, sir. You told us all about that before. Except last time it was me who'd killed three men, and she was the one who burned down the stable. Now, I agree we two are a dangerous pair and somebody ought to do something about it, but there's plenty of sheriffs and marshals, and we ain't making ourselves too concealed." His smile was the condescending smile one uses on a complete lunatic.

Beidler swung his eyes from one man to another. "I am X. Beidler," he stuttered.

The dentist said, "Yes, sir. So you said. I'm Jim Palmer, painless dentist, and I shan't introduce you to the others, because I think you should be leaving now."

Beidler said that he was a vigilante, but by then the dentist and the captain had his arms and were propelling him out of the room. Beidler said more on his way through the lobby, but none of it was believed.

The dentist and the captain were rather pleased with themselves, and each acquired a liking for the other, the liking of two men who had faced a tough situation and had not been found wanting.

The dentist took off his coat. He felt a warm glow, the warmth that assures us of our place in the world and the constant high regard of our fellows. Humbly, he waited for the captain to seat himself before he suggested that play should commence. He failed to notice the sweat darkening Bonnie's new gown and how her hands were kneading Slocum's shoulders restlessly.

The captain set his gold hunter on the baize table and announced that he couldn't play past three. Slocum said that he wouldn't cause any man to miss his sailing. The captain meant to correct him, meant to say that the *Rosebud* wouldn't sail until three days hence, but there was no reason to bring up a rude matter like that at a table of one's peers and friends. Slocum dealt slowly, more slowly than any other dealer, and the cards practically crawled off the deck. He dealt deliberately, because me have died for dealing seconds and at least as many for having the appearance.

The captain was a good card player, not terribly greedy, whose luck ran in short strings. He'd get three or four good hands in a row and then four or five bad ones. Apparently he knew his own patterns, because he bet well, taking a good price for his winning hands and dropping out cheap on the losers.

The dentist was greedy and lucky. Time after time he bet over his head, and the cards redeemed him. The dentist was half in the bag. His friend, the surveyor, was a fair player who was breaking even. Outside, it started to rain. The black waiter went around the room pulling curtains, but Slocum said that he wanted to watch the rain hit the muddy river. Like pellets from a shot tower, the rain lashed the river.

Slocum grinned to think of the Great Falls vigilantes on the trail tonight. The ground around Fort Benton was clay mud, which would turn into awful gumbo with a good rain, gumbo that would slow horses to a crawl, rain that would anger and weary and turn brave men foolish and quick ones slow. He wondered what X. Beidler was planning. Beidler had more nasty ideas than a mink in a woodchuck nest. Although he had sworn off firearms, Slocum wouldn't be surprised to find old X. armed again. He was a man in the grip of his occupation.

Slocum won a small pot with kings and a ten. The dentist groaned. He'd won a half dozen pots with a high card, and his ace had beat anything on the board. The dentist finished his brandy and called for the waiter to bring a fresh one.

Most of the other tables were empty, and the waiter was sweeping the baize and emptying the ashtrays. "With you in a minute, sir."

Three aimless drunks were at the bar, swapping quiet lies and listening to the rain. The damp was cold, which meant that summer was over.

Slocum squinted against the smoke from his cigar, looked at fives wired back to back, and said, "Well, gents, it's $50 to you."

Fifty dollars wasn't the highest bet anyone had made, but it was high. The surveyor folded. Slocum took the dentist and the captain for $100 each.

The next hand, he bet $200 on an ace high. The captain saw the bet and angrily raised it back. "Hell," he said. "My eights are good as an ace high."

The captain had a pair of eights showing. Disingenuously, he had a third eight in the hole; even if Slocum had paired the ace, the captain had a lockup hand. One more card to come. The captain stared at Slocum's ace and leaned forward to wink. "Between us gentlemen, sir, I don't think you have the pair."

Slocum returned the wink. He said, "Three hundred of yours, and $300 more."

The captain's heart jumped in his chest. There was more money on the table than he'd seen all night, and all of it belonged to John Slocum. Even if he lost, the captain would be even. The dentist would be down no more than $100.

Their thinking had changed. A hundred dollars didn't seem like much money. They had been blinded.

The woman stood behind Slocum's chair, a weary talisman. She wasn't watching the cards anymore or the flow of the gold.

First she rested her weight on one hip, then the other, and thought about some other place, some other time.

"Three eights, which beats your aces."

"Aces?"

The dentist crowed his triumph. "Three ladies, gents."
He reached for the stakes.

"Go slow, friend," Slocum said, spreading his heart
flush. Neither of the other players had seen it coming,
although they'd stared at the cards as if they were
messages marked "personal."

The captain drained his brandy. His eyes watered. He
dabbed at them. Already the dentist was dealing again.
Slocum's wall of gold was lined up before him in
battlements and towers.

"Play cards?" he purred.

The captain intended nothing more than politeness, a
few $5 bets before he went back to the *Rosebud* to bed.

Within three hands the bets were up again because
slowing down as abruptly as they had made them all
dizzy. Fifty, a hundred dollars. The surveyor watched it
all with a sort of amazement. He felt privileged to be part
of it.

The dentist threw in a bad hand. "You'll have to take
my marker," he said.

John Slocum paused long enough to let him know that
he didn't have to take anybody's marker, before he
murmured, "Sure, sure. I hate to see a game like this
break up."

Outside the rain had stopped. It hadn't been enough to
wet the roads much. The brown river fled through the
square of lamplight from their window. The waiter
brought more brandy and cigars and took away a double
eagle from John Slocum for his service. He had five of
them so far tonight and meant to stay here and stay
attentive so long as the high rollers were rolling. A man
could always sleep later.

Currency flowed across the table fitfully, currency and
scraps of paper from the painless dentist. The dentist

stopped drinking. Slocum still filled his glass a little each time. He cut back on the cigars, just chewing on them. The cards fluttered, and human language was reduced to "raise," "fold," "cards," "bump," and "call."

In a nearby chair, the waiter fell asleep.

Bonnie Slade pulled up a couple of chairs from another table and lay down across them.

An ugly mottled rash was forming on the dentist's cheeks and forehead.

The captain bore down. He did everything right. But John Slocum shaded him three times for every two times the captain won.

Scraps of paper, bank notes, gold coins—all took up residence behind the low wall of gold, like an untidy bird's nest that has been bricked in.

The river outside got bigger and grayer as the morning light came up. Captain Cooper opened his wallet and tossed a $20 bill on the table—his penalty for the last hand. He spoke with the weary edge of a man whose best hasn't been good enough. "That's it, Slocum. I believe you've cleaned me out."

The dentist said, "We can't play with only three of us."

"I'm a little weary myself," Slocum said.

"My God, I'm down $500," the dentist said. "I'll have to sell my tools to pay it off."

"Don't bitch," the captain snarled. "I'm down $1,000. And it's cash."

John Slocum looked at him for a long moment. The man's hands fumbled as he tried to light a new cigar.

The dentist said, "Let's go home."

"Wait a minute. Wait a minute," his friend cautioned him.

Slocum's hand pushed all the currency, all the IOUs,

and about half the gold toward the exhausted riverboat captain.

The captain's eyes looked their question.

"Passage money," Slocum explained.

"I told you," the captain said stupidly, "that first-class passage on the *Rosebud* is $30 for you and $30 for your wife."

"But that was on the boat leaving three days from now."

"Yes. That's right."

He toppled one of his golden towers toward Captain Cooper. "This is for passage right now."

The captain looked at the pile for a good while. He said, "I guess those hide dealers are going to have to give them back to the buffalo."

"Looks like you're in for a spell of painless dentistry."

The captain laughed, showing two rows of pretty good teeth, which the dentist didn't think was very funny.

The captain went down to the wharf. His crew would have to start getting steam up. The captain would talk to the hide dealers, but no more than he had to.

John Slocum went upstairs for the saddlebags. The saddlebags were almost empty except for filthy socks and underclothes. The food was all used up, along with half his grubstake. It all looked dirty lying there on the great brass bed he hadn't been able to use but had paid for. Bonnie Slade was up, but her eyes were half shut. He put his jacket over her shoulders, because it was likely to be a misty, cold morning, and she was a little weaker than she should have been.

The plaza in front of the hotel was deserted. The two horses they'd ridden so many miles to the north stood at the hitch rail, dozing. Their footfalls hurried across the street. Slocum's boots clicked on the cobblestones beside the wharves.

He could smell the *Rosebud* before her firebox glow stabbed through the fog, could smell the hides and her heavy plume of wood smoke. Captain Cooper was keeping his word.

He paused, listening, but didn't hear any hoofbeats. He helped the girl over the rail and nodded to Captain Cooper. The captain said that he wouldn't be shipping next year's hides out of Fort Benton, and John Slocum said that maybe he could make up the lost business in mining machinery, but he stopped, embarrassed because Captain Cooper had guessed how thoroughly he'd been fooled by a man who wanted nothing but an immediate steamer downriver. The captain's little smile told Slocum all that he needed to know.

"Cast off, stern. Cast off, bow."

The steam engine made a thumping sound, and the captain blew his whistle three sharp toots, which Slocum wished he hadn't. He waited until the *Rosebud* was well out from the dock before he took Bonnie Slade back to their cabin. She was asleep in the bunk before he had time to get her shoes off. He covered her with a quilt and went back on deck for a smoke.

The front of the boat was piled high with stacked hides, and he couldn't stand on the prow, although he would have liked to. He leaned against the stinking hides, unconcerned. They'd get riper as they went downriver, and there was no use worrying now.

He heard a noise. He tossed a match in the river and came down on one knee, turning with his Colt out. Then there was only the sound of his breathing.

"Don't shoot. I am unarmed."

X. Beidler crawled onto the top of the bale of hides,

maybe ten feet over his head. Beidler looked pretty rumpled.

Slocum cocked his Colt. He didn't mean to, but his thumb did it.

X. Beidler said, "I have money for passage. I wish to see the captain."

The mist on both sides of sidewheeler. The steady grumble of its pistons. Couldn't see a thing on either side of the *Rosebud*, couldn't even tell how wide the river was.

"I think this is it," Slocum said. He meant it.

X. Beidler threw up both hands in surrender as Slocum's Colt leveled at his head. The muzzle looked big enough for a small man to take up residence in.

A grin suddenly flickered across John Slocum's mouth. "X. Beidler," he said. "Jump or slide?"

X. Beidler jumped.